(11/26/18

ist

book of a _____.
The next is a third
of the way completed.

_Dennis Lann____

MW01042118

Building a Better Raymond

_____

Dennis Lanning

Building a Better Raymond
(#1 of Rebuilding a Life Series)
Copyright © 2018 by Dennis Lanning

ISBN: 978-1983686252

Other titles by Dennis Lanning:

The Inside-Out Church (2014)
Circus on the Square (2015)
Chips of Granite (2018)

Dedication

**To all who have built a better life,
by following Christ.**

ACKNOWLEDGMENTS

I'm thankful to Barry Giddens, a brother in writing. I was adrift when Tate Publishing closed its doors, and you helped me get back on track.

Nancy Faircloth did a great job of editing my manuscript. Thank you for a keen eye for a consistent plot, good grammar, and best word choices.

I'm always grateful for the support of my congregation at Marshallville United Methodist Church, and my best friends, a group known as "K5."

More important than all those previously mentioned is the undergirding love of my life and my wife of over forty years, Joy Lanning.

Please understand that God is more important to me than anything or anyone else. God called me to be a United Methodist pastor, and has called me to write Christian novels. God guides and sustains me in all that I do.

Chapter 1

Dinah was acting a little funny tonight.

Usually, when Ray spent the evening reading technical journals, she slipped in and out of the room. His petite, blonde wife would be making something in the kitchen, or watching TV in the bedroom, something like that. Tonight she sat in a chair across the room, flipping through a magazine.

"Feeling alright?" Ray asked, running his fingers through his black hair.

Dinah just shrugged her shoulders and continued leafing through the magazine.

He decided that she must be working through a problem she had at school. Second-graders had quirky personalities. Dinah always seemed to figure out a way to get the best out of each of her students.

Ray had studied a lot in recent months, doing his best to keep up with advances in vacuum cleaner technology. The particular article he was reading tonight addressed design challenges in producing robotic vacuum cleaners that could negotiate steps. General Cleaning's own robotic vacuum, Butler Ben, was as advanced as any, but Ray was determined to make Ben the first that could clean carpet on a staircase. He hoped to have the problem figured out within the next eight to ten months.

Dinah put down her magazine. "Ray, we've got to talk."

Without putting down his journal, he replied, "Go ahead, I'm listening."

"I want you to look at me, please. This is very important."

He frowned, then stuck an envelope in the journal and closed it. Hopefully, this would not be one of those long discussions on where to go on next year's vacation.

Looking directly into his hazel eyes, she said, "I'm leaving you, Ray. I've already talked to a lawyer. To put it bluntly,…you're just not very exciting anymore."

He was shocked. He didn't know what to say.

"I'm going to get ready for bed. School time comes early. Good night, Ray."

*****

Ray's appetite left him, and he dropped ten pounds in twenty days. A hundred and fifty-five pounds didn't do a good job of covering his six-foot frame. Days slipped by, and he couldn't remember much about the day before, or the day before that.

Dinah had packed up everything she wanted on one Saturday while he was at work, including four closets full of clothes and very little furniture. Her mother, Hazel, lived alone on the other side of Horner and was glad to make room for her only child.

Ray had no idea that a divorce could be finalized so fast. Dinah requested no alimony, and the couple had no children. She and Ray used the same lawyer, one they had used when they bought the house. Ray did not ask Dinah to help pay for the mortgage, and she wanted only five thousand dollars as her share of the accrued equity of the home.

They had wed on July 4, 2004. Ten years and three months of marriage seemed to leave little recorded history.

*****

General Cleaning had hired Ray Wright the day after he finished Eli Dayton College, in the same city of Horner, Georgia, and he had been there ever since. He had the title of "team manager," which meant he was responsible for a group of eight workers, assemblers of the famous Butler Ben vacuum. He loved his job.

"Ben" actually was not supposed to be a success. It was just a dead-end project assigned to Ray on the day he started his second week with General. The manager of product development, Arnie Rice, had given up on the little disc vacuum cleaner that was supposed to clean a home's carpet while the residents were away. Arnie decided that houses were too different, and there were too many things that could go wrong, to just turn an unsupervised vacuum cleaner loose in a house. Ray had patiently worked through the challenges, though, and now Butler Ben was the best-selling robotic vacuum cleaner made.

In a funny way, Dinah had been part of the success Ray had in developing Butler Ben. Ray frequently ate lunch at Darby's, on Main Street in Horner, where bubbly Dinah had worked while she attended college. Ray would order the Number Two meal, and sit alone in the corner booth, his mind absorbed with Butler Ben while he ate his lunch. Sometimes Dinah would stop by for a minute to chat, and Ray would run an idea by her that he had about the little vacuum cleaner. She always sounded encouraging, and always gave him an honest opinion.

The attraction between Ray and Dinah grew, and they started dating. They were married three years later when she finished at Eli Dayton. She found him to be a kind and steady man, dedicated to her and to his job. Ray loved Dinah's effervescent nature. She was just the spark his life needed.

Dinah was always busy, taking an art class or doing aerobics or learning French cooking. She even talked him into taking six months of ballroom dancing during their second year of marriage.

Life settled into a comfortable routine. She taught at Miller Elementary, just a couple blocks from the house, and he loved being the Butler Ben expert at General Cleaning. They lived in a three-bedroom ranch house in a quiet neighborhood.

Looking back now, Ray could see that he had gotten more and more into his work. This was 'the other woman' that drove a wedge between Dinah and Ray. He never stopped thinking about his job. He had no one to blame for the divorce but himself.

*****

Frank shifted his six-foot-four frame a little in the restaurant booth and leaned forward on his elbows. His gray hair and bushy eyebrows exuded wisdom.

"Look, just let her go, Ray. My wife dumped me ten years ago, and I just threw myself into my work here. In a few months, it'll be just another chapter in your life."

Frank Raleigh was one of the two founding partners of General Cleaning. He hired Ray right out of college, May 12, 2000. That was over fifteen years ago. Ray treasured the opinions of his tall, slim boss about nearly everything, but this particular word of wisdom didn't feel like the answer Ray needed. It was Ray's dedication to work that had contributed heavily to Dinah's departure a year ago.

"Frank, I don't know. Every comment card or letter we get from a Butler Ben customer, no matter how caustic, has something in it we can learn from. In the same way, Dinah and I were married ten years. I can't just forget all that. I've got to learn from the mistakes I made."

"The past is past, Ray. You can't let it cloud your future. Like I said, work gave me a reason to get out of bed every morning, after Millie left. You've got to have a purpose. I'm fine now. Next month, September 1, I will retire, and I'm going to go anywhere and do anything Frank wants."

*****

The Horner Herald was not the New York Times. He had never gotten into the habit of reading the New York Times, for the very reason that it had too much news. Since Ray was obsessed with finishing any periodical he picked up, the Herald was more to his liking. Fifteen minutes would suffice for perusing the local paper.

Only Chuck Burden's column stood between Ray and the complete reading of today's Herald. His eyes jumped to the task.

Groovin'

You know, doing everything the same today as yesterday is a good thing. So much of life is undependable and changeable; it's good to know something is steady. When you manage to get everyday life into a routine, you can more easily handle the odd things that go wrong.

At least that's the theory people live by. Like most theories, it has to be tried to see if it really works. If it does, we've got a "law," like the Law of Gravity or Newton's Laws of Motion (a body at rest tends to stay at rest, and a body in motion tends to stay in motion). Does the theory work, "If most of life is kept the same, change is easier to handle"?

There is much discussion as to whether this theory concerning change is true. Some say it's never really been tested, since no one has ever gotten all their ducks in a row. Others say it's obviously true.

I live by an alternate theory: Since God does not change, anchor yourself to him, and you can handle anything that comes up. Works for me, every time.

That sounded like Frank's idea: Keep focused on your work, and you'll be able to handle change, change as in divorce. According to Chuck Burden, nobody knew if that really worked.

What does he mean, "Since God does not change, anchor yourself to him"? Ray became a Christian when he was sixteen, so he guessed he was "anchored." Then again, it seemed like the rope attached to the anchor must be mighty long, and mighty slack.

*****

Chapter 2

He hated country music. No, that's not true. Ray hated any loud music in the neighborhood that intruded on his reading. It just happened that the Lansing teenager next door played country music when he washed his Mustang, so tonight Ray hated country music.

Other nights Ray hated other music. Sarah Hansen's new boyfriend was into rap music. He would park in the Hansen's driveway across the street a couple evenings a week and chat with Sarah, rap music blaring. So last night it was rap music that Ray hated.

When Dinah lived here, loud music was not a problem. All the kids loved Dinah. She would step outside, locate the source of the music, then go make a visit. She would sing and dance with the kids, just like someone their own age. Then she would ask if the music wasn't a tad too loud. When she came back home, the music would have decreased to a much more pleasant level.

Alright, that's enough. Ray decided to go out for a snack. Maybe the neighborhood would be quieter when he got back.

"Hey, Mr. Wright," called out Rob Lansing. As Ray walked toward his own white Ford Focus, the brown-haired, lanky teen with the loud country music sauntered over to chat. "Haven't seen your wife lately. Has she gone on a trip or something?"

"No, actually she's living with her mother now. We got a divorce about a year ago." Ray fumbled with his keys. He wasn't very good at small talk, though he used to be. He certainly wasn't good at chatting about his divorce.

"Oh, man, I'm sorry. Must be hard, living alone and all. Maybe we can invite you over, next time Dad grills steaks. He's in love with his gas grill."

"Thank you. That would be great. I never have taken the time to master any kind of cooking."

"Well, see you around. Guess I'd better go in and hit the books. Got a history test tomorrow." Rob Lansing waved, smiled, and stuck his head in his car to turn off the country music station.

*****

Darby's was now in its eighteenth year of operation. Stanley Darby had worked in a Subway sandwich franchise while in high school, then worked his way up to manager after he entered college. After two years and an associate degree in business at Eli Dayton, Stanley had saved enough money to open his own sandwich shop.

Darby's started small, a fifteen-foot wide and forty-foot deep storefront in a strip shopping mall. Customers really took to Stanley's inventive burger and sub sandwich items. When a print shop foreclosed on Main Street in Horner, he took out a loan and moved to the new location, sixteen years ago.

Tonight the television that hung high on the wall in the corner of Darby's was showing a vinyl siding commercial when Ray came in midway through the six o'clock news.

"You look like a man who needs a large chocolate shake and an order of fries,"said Stanley. "Ray, I know you like a book. Am I right?"

"Yes, sir," he answered. "I must have had that look on my face. Stan, I'll just sit here at the counter."

Stanley nodded, and took Ray's order to the kitchen.

No one else was sitting at the counter tonight. Glancing around, he saw several families of three or four at tables, plus several couples seated at booths. He was the odd one. The world was not oriented toward single persons.

When he was married to Dinah, he never ate alone. Looking back, he now wondered if she had felt alone, since he was always thinking or talking about work. No, whenever they were out at a restaurant or shopping, Dinah was making conversation with everyone nearby. He was the one that was alone, in his own little world.

"Local residents are upset with Planning and Zoning for allowing a new nightspot near an east side residential section," announced the news anchor. "The Landon Acres area has been a family-friendly community for decades, say homeowners there. The new Whitney's Wild Nights would bring increased traffic, higher noise levels, and nearly a dozen new parking lot lights. More on this story at eleven."

The pudgy proprietor set Ray's shake and fries down on the counter. "There you go, Raymond."

"Looks great, Stanley. Thanks."

"So what do you think? Are you for or against the new Whitney's?"

Ray looked up at the proprietor. "I don't know. Where is it going to be?"

Stanley paused several seconds, staring at Ray. "Are you kidding? You must be working too hard. Ray, it will be about a block from your house. Your neighbors talk about it every day in here."

Ray shrugged. "To each his own. I guess if they don't bother me, I won't bother them."

Stanley shook his graying head and stepped back to the kitchen.

*****

As he drove home, Ray wondered about his plan for getting through the divorce. He was trying his best to throw himself even more into his work. He got to General Cleaning about 6:45 now, and was often the last to leave at 6:00 or 6:15. With such long hours, one would think he'd be making dramatic advances in Butler Ben designs, but the truth was that he couldn't focus like he used to.

With Dinah gone, there were more details to worry about, like meals and laundry and paying bills. There was no one to remind him to call his mother, or to get his car's oil changed. He was the one who had to make sure the alarm clock was set and the dishwasher was run.

Truth be told, Ray missed her. Living alone was lonely. Maybe working harder was not the answer. Still, it had worked for Frank Raleigh. He'd try a little bit longer. Maybe a year wasn't long enough.

Ray decided to take a detour on the way home. He wanted to see just where the new Whitney's Wild Nights was going to be located. His friend Stanley had indicated it was under construction on Broad Avenue, right by the interstate.

He drove past his regular turnoff, where he would go a block south and then turn on Maple, and instead continued on Broad. Passing under I-75, he began looking for signs of construction. He could see nothing that looked new or incomplete, nothing being built. After a mile, Ray turned around and headed back, still not finding the Whitney's construction site.

He passed under the interstate again and headed home. Suddenly he saw it. A billboard above a construction site read, "Coming Soon! No better music or dancing anywhere! Whitney's Wild Nights is for you!"

The new business would be a hundred feet from his back door.

*****

Raymond Wright loved October. The annual Home Electronics Expo began in Nashville on the third Monday of that month each year. For any electronics inventor or designer of household appliances, the Nashville show defined their calendar. Nashville capped one year and began the next.

General Cleaning always buzzed in September and October, getting ready to wow the industry with vacuum cleaner advances that were still on the drawing board, but ready to come off the production line "very soon." The intent was to make competitors feel woefully behind.

Ray was eager to get to work. His dental appointment made him mid-morning arriving on the job.

Something seemed amiss today, though. The calendar proclaimed October, but General Cleaning whispered instead of buzzed. Managers sat in their offices with doors closed. Production workers talked quietly in small clusters.

Ray stopped at the office of Tom Sullivan. Tom was one of the two founding partners of General

Cleaning. He took on the title of President when Frank Raleigh retired last month.

"Good morning, Brenda," Ray said cheerfully to Mr. Sullivan's red-haired secretary. "What's going on around here? The place is quiet. Did somebody die?"

The secretary stared at Ray, struggling to speak. Something definitely was wrong.

Brenda picked up her phone and pressed a button. "Mr. Sullivan, could you speak to Ray Wright? He hasn't heard. Thank you, I'll send him in."

Turning to Raymond, she said, "Ray, I'll let Mr. Sullivan fill you in. I just can't."

Puzzled, he walked into Tom's office. Tom turned from staring out the window.

"Morning, Ray. Have a seat. We're going to close at noon for the day. Nobody is getting anything done."

"Wow. What in the world is going on?"

Tom Sullivan looked down at his desk a few seconds, turning a pen over and over in his fingers. "It's Frank, Ray. He died this morning, just after eight, out on the golf course."

He stared, wide-eyed, at the short, lean company president. It couldn't be. Frank looked great a month ago at his retirement celebration.

"Tom, I had no idea he was sick. He looked real good, the last time I saw him."

"Frank's doctor is a friend of mine, and we talked just a few minutes ago. He said he sees this far too often, in men especially. They pour themselves into their work and then, when they retire, they suddenly have no stress and no responsibility. They don't feel needed. Too many drop dead in less than six months."

Ray thought, *And here I am, doing my best to be like Frank.*

*****

On an unseasonably warm day in October, 2015, several dozen people gathered at the graveside of Frank Raleigh. Kind and generous words were spoken, but for those that knew him well, it could all be summed up in one short phrase: Frank was a workaholic. Much of General Cleaning's success in the residential cleaning appliance industry could be traced to his years of determined research and innovation. The long work hours had also been largely responsible for his divorce and estranged children.

Ray Wright left the funeral deeply troubled. He had a lot in common with Frank Raleigh. Unless he made some very fundamental changes in his lifestyle, and soon, he could see that his future would be much shorter than he had originally planned.

*****

Chuck Burden's newspaper column caught his attention after supper that night. Somehow it was a message to him personally, though Ray had never met the man.

Moving the Furniture

I guess I've always been the kind of person who likes to rearrange the furniture. I like to move chairs and bookcases and things, to give myself a fresh look at what I've got around me. I mean, I can stand things where they are for a while, maybe years, but then I've got to finally break out and move the furniture.

My brother was not necessarily like that, and as long as we shared a bedroom, things stayed pretty much the same. I remember we unstacked the bunk beds for awhile, but I don't remember much furniture moving besides that. When my brother joined the Air Force, you can believe things found themselves in new places pretty quickly.

Am I like that in my Christian life? Well, maybe a little. Mostly, though, I kind of like to get into a groove, and stay there. I want a regular routine, regular devotional practices, pray the same kind of words, etc.

It's funny, though, God is the same today, yesterday and forever, right? In the beginning, God was creative, so I ought to expect him to still be that way. Somehow, he's always pulling the rug out from under me, showing me new things, taking me new places, taking me out of my rut, and generally turning the world upside down.

God's always rearranging the furniture. And he'll keep on doing it until, well, until we've been made in the image of his dear son.

It was time for Ray to move furniture, and not just in some spiritual way. Life was just not working. The past year had rushed by, with Ray living in a daze.

He determined to put his house on the market and start over someplace else. It was time to rebuild Raymond. Maybe he could build a little better this time.

*****

Chapter 3

"Stewart Realty. This is Betty Stewart. How can I help you?"

He had expected a secretary to answer. Ray thought he'd have a few more seconds to formulate his first few sentences.

"Good morning, ma'am. My name is Raymond Wright. I want to sell my house." He meant to say he was considering selling his house.

"Please call me Betty. I am so glad you chose Stewart Realty. Raymond, I'll need to come see your property, of course, but let me get some basic information while I have you on the phone, alright?"

"Yes, that's fine."

"Address?"

"Most people address me as Ray."

There was a slight pause on Betty's side of the conversation.

"Where do you live, Ray?"

"I'm still living in the house I'm wanting to sell."

Another pause.

"Ray, please give me the address of the house you want to sell, the one you live in."

"Oh. Sorry. The address is 315 Maple Drive, Horner."

"That would be in the Landon Acres section. Brick?"

Ray replied, "Most of them are. My house is."

"Do you know how many square feet in your house?"

"It's thirty by sixty, Betty, plus a two-car garage. The house is on a two-acre lot."

"That's a pretty big lot for Landon Acres. Alright. I will need to see the house, and get a photograph to help with the advertising. I would assume you will need a little time to straighten things. How soon might I come by? Today is Saturday." Ray could hear Betty Stewart flipping calendar pages.

"Right now would be a great time. I always keep things in good order." He wondered why anyone would want to view a house that didn't look lived in.

"Well, certainly, that will be fine. I'll be there in ten minutes."

*****

A white Lexus pulled up to the curb in front of 315 Maple Drive, and a tall, sturdy brunette stepped out of the car.

Immediately, she took a tablet computer from her large handbag. Using the top of the Lexus as a makeshift tripod, she quickly took several pictures of the front of Ray's house.

He stepped to the front door and walked down the sidewalk toward the car. "You must be the realtor."

Betty laughed. "I'll bet you're glad. I'm either Betty Stewart or a private investigator."

Ray extended his hand. "I'm pleased to meet you, Betty. Need any more pictures?"

She shook his hand firmly. "Actually, I'd like to walk through your house and record it all on video. But I'll let you show me around first. Is your family here?"

"I'm afraid I am the entire family. My wife and I recently divorced."

"Oh, dear, I'm so sorry. Is she co-owner of the property?"

He shook his head, "No, it's all mine. I paid Dinah for her part of the equity."

Thirty minutes later, the realtor headed for her car. "Raymond, your house is in great condition, and your asking price should garner a lot of attention. The property really only has one significant drawback, and that may make it difficult for me to find a buyer."

Ray felt a sudden wave of disappointment. "Is it something I can have repaired without much trouble?"

"I'm afraid not." Betty got in her Lexus and lowered the window. "The problem is your proximity to the new nightspot. Few people would want to live just a hundred feet from Whitney's Wild Nights."

"Does that mean I might be waiting several weeks before it sells?" Ray asked.

"It could be quite a bit longer."

*****

Darby's made some of the best sub sandwiches in Horner. Ray usually ordered the foot-long cold cut combo, with a side of slaw and unsweetened tea. He never understood why his carryout order included packets of salt and pepper.

After a few bites, Ray started looking around his kitchen. When the house sold, he'd have a lot of sorting to do. Even though everything was orderly and in its proper place, the house contained twice as much of everything that a bachelor would ever use. He might as well start going through stuff, just to get ahead of the game.

But where would he go? In his magnificent plan to make a fresh start in life, Ray had not yet considered where this new start would take place. Somewhere else in Horner? Maybe he should consider one of the small towns in the area. There was no question that he would continue at General Cleaning.

Everybody at the office knew that Frank Raleigh's house was for sale, most agreeing that it could be bought at a bargain price. Of course, that was too big a house for Ray, with much too big a yard.

Stanley Darby's grandma had lived in nearby Buckner before she moved to assisted living two years ago. When she died last year, Stanley inherited her home. Surely that house had sold by now.

He would let himself be guided by Betty Stewart when and if Ray's Horner house sold. He needed other major changes besides where he called home. He was going to find a life after Dinah. He was determined to build a better Raymond.

*****

He just had to learn to cook. Eating cereal for breakfast, then eating frozen dinners or restaurant food for lunch and supper wasn't working. His clothes were not fitting well anymore, and he suspected it was not entirely due to his limited laundering skills.

Tonight Ray endeavored to conquer fabricating spaghetti. How difficult could it be? Just put noodles in boiling water, and let them cook until tender. Actually, there was a little more to it. He found out last time that spaghetti noodles stick together in one big mass if they are not stirred. He wouldn't make that mistake again.

Ray put his new colander in the sink. When the noodles were tender, he poured the contents of the pot into the colander. Placing the pot back on the stove, he poured in the jar of spaghetti sauce. He asked out loud, "Why use two pots?", feeling a bit smug.

He looked to the right, and saw an unopened can of green beans. "Oh. I guess I will need another pot for the green beans."

In a few minutes, his supper was ready. A hot plate of spaghetti with meat sauce occupied his customary end of the kitchen table. Next to it was a yellow bowl with the green beans, adjacent to a container of cole slaw from the grocery store deli.

I'm going to be alright, he thought as he ate his second bite of spaghetti. *I can cook. I've taught myself to do the laundry, and I can keep an exceptionally clean house.* He decided that he was getting the hang of being a single person.

Then he tasted the beans. They were the worst he'd ever had! What in the world had happened?

The empty can sat on the counter. Below the words, "Green Beans" was another line that said, in red ink, "No Salt Added."

*****

"Hello?"

"This is Mrs. Rex Wright calling for Raymond Wright. Has anybody seen him lately?"

Ray shook his head. "Mom, I meant to call you a couple weeks ago. How long has it been? A month? I'll try to call you more often. I know you worry about me."

32

Caroline answered sweetly, "Worry? Just because I haven't heard from my oldest son in over two months? No, the Lord tells us not to worry about anything. I would like to hear from you a little more often, though. I care about what goes on in your life, son."

"I'm okay, Mom. Life is an adventure. I'm learning new things, like washing clothes and the proper way to load a dishwasher."

"No pink underwear yet?" his mom asked skeptically.

"Oh, maybe one time," said Ray, "but I learned from my mistake. Never again."

"How is my old Ford doing?"

Ray always bought his mother's old car when she bought a new one, giving her much more than a dealer would. "Jessie Belle is running as good as ever, Mom. They say you always get a good used car when you buy it from a little old lady that just drives it to church and back."

"Who are you calling old? Seventy is not old. And little? Half my Sunday School class is smaller than me. Five foot nine is not little."

His mother paused for a moment, and Ray knew exactly what was coming next. He decided to beat her to the punch. "I think it's time for you to buy a new car, Mom. You've had that Chevy for five years now. I'm ready to sell Jessie Bell, if you'll part with the car you're driving now."

"Raymond, it is so generous of you to offer to buy my car. I really have been thinking of getting something newer. Your sister and brother always want me to have a dependable car, and five years with a vehicle is as far as I should probably chance it."

"How about a red car this time, Mom?" He stifled a laugh. Caroline Wright never bought any color car but white.

"What! No, I read years ago that a white car shows up better than any other color. People need to see me coming and stay in their own lane. Now, this car is in great shape, and I've got all the repair records. I think it's worth at least five thousand dollars."

Ray did not make a sound for a full thirty seconds. This was fun.

"Son, are you still there? You need to pay me at least four thousand, not a cent less."

"Mom."

"Not a cent less."

Ray paused for another few seconds. "Mom, I couldn't sleep at night if I paid you four thousand dollars for that car. Ten thousand dollars, take it or leave it."

Caroline Wright shouted, "Sold! When can you pick it up?"

*****

Ray had only Chuck Burden's column left to read in this week's Horner Herald.

Flying Carpet

Just when you think you've got a plan for your life, you come to a 'flying carpet moment.' That's what I call it when the rug gets pulled out from under you.

The Bible has all kinds of advice for times like that, from "Don't worry about tomorrow," in Matthew 6, to "Count the cost before you jump into anything," in Luke 14, to "Don't set your future plans in concrete," in James 4.

Wait! Not all that advice sounds like it goes together. How is a person supposed to plan for the future?

As I read it, God encourages us to get the facts and figures before we start on our plans, then go ahead, keeping in mind that most things don't work out quite the way we think they will.

And, instead of worrying, pray. That is, when riding a flying carpet, it's good to have something to hold on to, and that's God.

*****

Chapter 4

It had been a week since Ray put his house up for sale. The realtor had suggested they initially set the price at two hundred ninety-five thousand, leaving room to reduce the price if the house lingered on the market over a year. Ray would be glad to come down more on the price, if it meant selling a lot sooner.

He had not yet begun to pack or sort through his belongings. Maybe he should aim at packing up a room each month, starting with the garage.

The kitchen telephone rang, scaring Ray so much that he slopped half his coffee on the floor. He hadn't realized his ear was only inches from the phone. Dodging the spill, he quickly answered the call.

"Raymond? This is Betty Stewart. I'm sorry to call before nine on a Saturday. How are you today?"

"Fine, thank you, Betty. I'm usually up by six on Saturdays, so don't be afraid to call early. What can I do for you?" *Surely she doesn't want to lower the price already,* Ray tried to assure himself.

"Raymond, I'd like to bring a customer by to see your house today. When would be a good time? I think he would prefer this morning, if possible."

"How about ten, Betty?" he answered. "That will give me an hour to wash my breakfast dishes and run an errand."

Betty Stewart sounded surprised. "Don't you want to put some things away or straighten up a bit? You need to make the best impression. Remember, your house may be hard to sell."

"No problem, Betty. I'm the kind that keeps things orderly even when I'm not expecting company."

He was never expecting company.

* * * * *

Ray had just returned from the dry cleaner when Betty Stewart's white Lexus pulled up to the curb in front of the house. He quickly hung the clothes in the hall closet and met Betty on the front walk.

Accompanying her was a tall, slim man in jeans and a red, button-up shirt. His hair was brown with gray at the temples.

"Raymond," Betty started, "I'd like you to meet Bill Whitney. He called me yesterday to inquire about available homes in this part of town, and I immediately knew he had to see yours. Bill, this is Ray Wright."

The two men smiled and shook hands. "What can I show you first, Mr. Whitney?" said Ray.

"Could I show him around, Ray?" Betty quickly inserted. "I can't wait to show him all the special things about your home." Both men nodded, and Betty headed for the door.

*****

"The house is everything I need, Ms. Stewart," said Bill Whitney. "I hope we can find a price we can agree on."

Ray started to speak, but Betty gently squeezed his arm. He decided that meant she would handle the negotiations.

"What price range did you have in mind, Mr. Whitney? Raymond and I have discussed some figures. I'm sure we can find common ground."

"As you know, Ms. Stewart, my place of business is within walking distance, so that counts for a lot. The neighbors seem to take pride in their homes, and I really like that. This house is in great shape, I'll have to say. Would you consider three hundred ten?"

Ray did all he could to keep a calm expression on his face. *She had better say yes!*

"That's a little different than we had in mind, actually. Three twenty-five was the limit we'd talked about."

Bill Whitney turned his back to Betty and Ray. Was he leaving?

Betty looked at Ray and held her finger to her mouth, reminding him to keep quiet.

Turning back to them, Bill Whitney said, "I think I could be happy with three hundred twenty thousand, and I'd pay the closing costs. Can we compromise with that? And I'd like to move in by the middle of next month."

Betty looked at Ray, who gave a little nod, and it was done.

*****

Stop daydreaming, Ray.

He shook his head a little, and looked at his plate. Wow, Stanley had outdone himself with this burger. The cheese and jalapenos peeked out from under a slice of red ripe tomato, interrupted by drizzles of that special sauce found only at Darby's. Ray realized he was wasting perfection, and grabbed the sandwich with both hands.

Stanley snuck a glance at his long-time customer every few minutes. He knew something big was distracting Ray today. Usually the Hot Almighty Burger was gone in less than five minutes.

The proprietor took a moment to ease over to Ray's table. "How's the burger today, pal?"

"Magnificent. You've hit perfection today, Stanley. Amazing burger."

"Yeah? You sure are making it last. Ray, you must have something eating you, or you'd be swallowing that sandwich a whole lot faster."

"You know me too well, old friend. I'll try to pay more attention to the project at hand."

Stanley sat down across from Ray. "I'll bet you're worried about your house. Look, you've got to be patient. It may take months to sell. The real estate market is slow right now around here."

Ray put his burger down, wiped his fingers on a napkin, and folded his hands in front of him. "You're partly right, Stanley. It's the house I'm worried about, but not about selling it. The realtor brought a customer by this morning for the first time, and he bought it right away. He even paid more than I had wanted to get out of it."

Stanley sat up straight. "Wow! Are you kidding? That's incredible. I wish I had that problem."

"Yeah, but the problem is, the new owner will be moving in about three weeks from now, and I don't have a place to live. I haven't even begun to look for a house."

"Ray, I've got just the opposite problem. My grandmother died a year ago and left me her house, and nobody has even looked at it yet. Maybe we can solve each other's problem."

*****

A week ago he had decided to sell his house and start living differently. This morning, his house sold, and he needed to be out in three weeks. Now Ray was on his way to look at a new house in a town he had never stepped foot in. Everything was moving too fast. This was insane.

No, insanity is doing the same things, the same way, and expecting different results. This was actually a step in the right direction.

"You'll come into Buckner on Sixth Street," Stanley told him. "Turn right at the Shell station, just past the city limits sign. Go to Third Street and turn left. It's 107 West Third Street, on the left, brick, nice front porch."

Ray saw the Shell station coming up on his left as he passed the Buckner City Limits sign. Another sign informed him that the "business district" was straight ahead. Ray turned right on Elm, drove three blocks, then turned left on Third Street, just past the sign for St. John Community Church.

Creeping down the street, he carefully peered at each building to spy its house number. Ray pulled up to the curb across from 107 West Third Street and let the white Ford Focus idle.

So this was Stanley's grandmother's house. He wondered if Grandma had emanated the same presence as this house, solid but homey.

Even with a wide front porch, the brick house looked very square. The roof sloped up from all four sides to a high center point. No chimney was evident, nor any gables. Each side of the building looked to be about thirty-five feet.

The boxwoods in front of the house sported no leaves, only a tightly-woven mass of bare branches. At their base was a thick carpet of pine straw, adequate to deter weeds but evidently of no help in keeping the shrubs alive.

He pulled into the wide concrete driveway and stopped inside the two-car garage connected to the house by a short covered walkway.

Ray dug in his pocket for the house keys. Nothing so far had overly impressed him about the building. Then again, Ray had no idea what he needed or was looking for. He needed a change, and perhaps whatever home he settled on would nudge him in the right direction.

*****

"So, what did you think of my grandmother's house?"

"Stanley, let me tell you something very important first." Ray paused. He leisurely picked up a menu.

Stanley stood by silently, unable to stand completely still. He could tell that Ray had found something wrong with the house.

"Well, Ray, what is it? Tell it to me straight."

Ray put down the menu and looked Stanley in the eye. "Make it a hot ham and cheese this time, with fries and a Coke. I've neglected that sandwich, and that's a shame. You make it better than anybody in town."

Stanley stared at Ray for a second, mumbled something, then walked to the kitchen. Ray looked down and covered his mouth with his hand, so that Stanley wouldn't see the grin on his face.

A few minutes later, Stanley returned with Ray's order. Ray slid the house keys across the counter to Stanley.

"So, what did you think of the house?"

Ray took a bite of the sandwich and shrugged. After a sip of his drink, he replied, "I guess it's fine. I'm not really sure what I'm looking for. Maybe after I look at another house or two, could be it'll be the best I've seen."

"Look, Ray, buddy, I'll make you a good deal. I don't need another house to look after, especially not in another town. This restaurant keeps me busy six days a week."

Ray took another bite of the ham and cheese and drummed his fingers on the counter.

"Grandma's house is in great shape. I guess you saw that. It's worth a hundred and fifty to a hundred and seventy-five thousand. Ray, let's settle on a hundred thousand even. You can stop looking, and save yourself a lot of time and trouble. I really want to sell you that house."

Ray chewed a little more on his sandwich, then reached over to retrieve the house keys, still on the counter. "That's a mighty good offer. Let me look at it again tomorrow. I'll call you tomorrow night."

*****

Chapter 5

For the second day in a row Raymond Wright parked in the garage of 107 West Third Street in Buckner. This time he walked up to the front porch of the house. A cocker spaniel paused as it walked past, like a policeman on foot patrol. He remembered seeing the same dog the day before.

What a great porch! If Ray liked sitting in a rocking chair on a front porch and speaking to neighbors as they walked by, this would be the perfect place. *I need to become that kind of person. I'm trying to build a better Raymond.* The porch extended across the entire front of the house, six or seven feet deep.

Ray stepped inside the first room. It seemed to be a combination of kitchen and dining area and den. It, too, went all the way across the house. Even without furniture he could see, by the location of the cabinets and sink, that the kitchen was on the right, with an outside door to the garage.

The master bedroom and bath were behind the kitchen, on the right side of a central hall. The second bedroom was on the left, behind the den, and then another full bath. A smaller room behind that must have been a reading room or library, evidenced by walls full of windows and bookshelves.

It was a simple house, maybe two-thirds the size of the house he was selling in Horner. Would it be a good place to make a fresh start?

Stanley had proclaimed, "You'll like Buckner. My grandmother lived there her whole life. It's real peaceful." There was probably a good reason Stanley had not been able to sell his grandmother's house. When someone describes a town as 'peaceful,' that usually means 'dead.'

Ray yearned for change in his life, but everything whizzed along at supersonic speed. He read something about that a few days ago, didn't he? Oh, yeah, Chuck Burden's column last week talked about riding a flying carpet. Seems his bottom line had been, "When riding a flying carpet, it's good to have something to hold on to, and that's God."

God was out there somewhere. *Where do I find a handhold?*

Maybe it had been too long since Ray had really prayed. Then again, what's fifteen years to a God who's been around forever? "Dear God," he said, out loud with his eyes wide open, "I'm starting over. I think I'll buy this house. Does that sound okay?"

Maybe God would help him plant his feet in the right place.

*****

Even though Ray had been at General Cleaning for fifteen years, it still made him a little nervous when he was told the boss wanted to see him. Tom Sullivan was a great friend, and always had good things to say about Ray's work. Still, Tom was the boss, the company president, and the sole remaining founder since Frank's retirement and subsequent demise.

Brenda hit the intercom button. "Tom, Ray Wright is here. Yes, I'll send him in."

As Ray entered the president's office, Tom Sullivan rose to shake his hand. "Have a seat, Ray. If you don't mind, push the door to." Though Tom was smiling, nothing so far had calmed Ray's nerves.

The boss's desk was covered with stacks of paper. A wrapper with a half-eaten breakfast biscuit sat on the only uncluttered space. Tom's favorite blue coffee mug sat atop the tallest stack.

"Tom, what's happened in here? You must be swamped. I've never seen more than a couple pieces of paper on your desk before." Ray wondered if he spoke too soon; perhaps there was a logical reason for the mess. Maybe Tom was reorganizing a filing cabinet.

Tom shook his head and looked down. "You are absolutely right. I've never felt so far behind with my work. But I've got a plan. It'll all get done."

Ray leaned forward in his chair. "I was told you wanted to see me. Is this a good time?"

"Glad you came by so promptly. Yeah, I guess you could say I've got good news and bad news for you, Ray."

Again, Tom had not said anything to ease Ray's nerves.

"I'll tell you the bad news first. You're doing great work, as always. You've been one of our best hires ever. I guess Frank gets the credit for that.

"I've been looking at your notes on your latest project, trying to figure out how our Butler Ben can be made to navigate steps in a house. Looks like a tough concept."

Ray fidgeted a little. "I'm hoping for a breakthrough soon. I need to figure out how to shift the center of gravity on the little disk vacuum cleaner, so that it doesn't skip a step and just tumble down to the bottom. You're right, it's tough."

Tom smiled just a little. "I guess that's the bad news. As of today, I want you to quit working on the project. No more trying to make Butler Ben clean stairs. We've put enough time into this, and I don't see that it would become a huge selling point."

Ray couldn't help but frown. A lot of hours of hard thinking were being tossed out the window, but it was Tom Sullivan's decision. He was the boss. "If you're sure, Tom, then okay, I'll quit immediately on that. I'll file my notes, in case some of the concepts apply to something else later on."

"That's good, Ray. I know you are not one to quit on anything. You'll have to trust me on this.

"And now the good news." Tom paused several seconds, not as much for anticipation as to make a clean break from the earlier conversation.

Ray thought, *I'll bet he's taking me to lunch.*

"It's about my desk." Tom smiled, and again paused for several seconds. "I need help. I've had too much to do since Frank retired. I keep falling farther behind.

"General Cleaning has never had a vice-president, but now is the time. Ray, I need you to take that position."

He was shocked. "What would I be asked to do?"

Tom shifted in his chair. "We can make adjustments, but this is what I'm thinking so far: Number one, you would be my link to the other employees. Second, you would be charged with making sure we put out the best quality product of any household appliance maker in the country. I would also want to be assured our employees have everything they need to stay here for their whole careers.

"You'd need to take some management classes, which you could do online, three or four hours every afternoon for awhile, probably some ongoing reading after that."

Ray responded, "General Cleaning has always been a close-knit family. I can see how keeping that unity by retaining employees longer would help us produce high-quality products."

"Along those same lines," added Tom, "I want you to promise me you'll keep your hours reasonable. Even my vice-president needs to work no more than forty-five hours a week. That may be hard for you, I know. You're a lot like Frank Raleigh."

Ray didn't want his only focus in life to be his job. He was trying to not end up like Frank, with no other life after he retired. But forty-five hours?

"Oh, I didn't mention one more thing. Your pay would be an even hundred thousand to start, up twenty from what you're making now. As I get closer to retirement, I'll increase it as you take on more of my responsibilities.

"Think about this overnight, Ray. If you don't want to take on the vice-president position, I'll understand. You are the only one I'm considering for this. I really could use your help."

*****

November 14, 2015, was looming large. There were only fifteen days left before Ray would turn his house over to the owner of Whitney's Wild Nights. Ray had agreed to buy Stanley's house in

Buckner, and for the past few days a cleaning service had been scouring it from top to bottom.

Next week's vacation would be used to fly to upstate New York to get his mom's five-year-old Chevy Malibu and drive it back. He'd have to get her situated in a new vehicle, though she usually already knew what kind of car she wanted next.

With new responsibilities at work, packing for the move had been put on the back burner. Finally, Ray was starting to get a handle on what to do as General Cleaning's new VP, so now he could focus on moving.

The bottom line was that he needed to get this house packed tomorrow and Sunday.

The music from outside made it difficult to concentrate. It was country, so it likely was emanating from Rob Lansing's car. Maybe Ray should go ask the kid to lower the volume.

Wait! Maybe the neighbor boy would like to make some money by helping him pack. It could be kept simple. Ray could buy lots of boxes of various sizes, rolls of bubble wrap, then let Rob roll each item in bubble wrap and stuff it in a box. Each box would be labeled as to what room the contents came from. Ray could decide, once he got to Buckner, where everything would go in the new house.

It seemed like a reasonable plan, if Rob was willing.

*****

"I don't know. That's pretty intense physical labor, especially if I have to pack it all in two days or less. How about ten bucks an hour instead of eight? And bring me a pizza for lunch and maybe a burger and fries for supper."

Rob Lansing went back to the task of washing his car, moving in a steady rhythm that matched the radio music.

Ray stuck his hands in his pockets and looked off into the distance. How did he know Rob would do a good job? He didn't. A professional moving company would charge fifteen dollars an hour, probably two hundred bucks minimum, but he might not be able to get them on such short notice.

On the other hand, Ray would be packing other things in the same house, and could watch over the kid. He didn't own many things that couldn't be replaced if they got broken.

"Rob, I think you would do a good job. I'll make the deal on one condition."

The teen stopped washing his car and looked at Raymond Wright. "What's the condition?"

Ray responded, "That you turn down the music on your car radio for the rest of the night."

Rob smiled, reached into his car, and turned the radio completely off.

*****

Ray looked forward to Chuck Burden's column in the Horner Herald. He seemed to have a grasp on how to handle life.

Talk to Me

It's amazing how backward you need to be, to be a good conversationalist. Let me explain what I mean.

Theoretically, a good conversationalist knows interesting little things to say. They can make small talk about the weather, current events, the price of groceries, or whatever. Friend, that's not really what it takes.

Who is it you really enjoy talking to? It's someone who is interested in you. It's somebody that asks questions about you, and listens to what you say. So, obviously, to be a good conversationalist, your conversation should be about the other person.

Can you see the importance of that old, old Bible principle, "Love your neighbor as yourself"? We all want to be listened to, to have someone hear our story. Being a good conversationalist takes loving the other person.

Isn't it strange? If you listen well, folks will praise your skill at conversation.

*****

Chapter 6

"Thirty-seven years old, Raymond, and you're finally learning to cook. Dinah must have done everything for you. At least you can keep your house clean." Caroline Wright took another sip of coffee and stretched her long legs out in front of her favorite living room chair.

"I got that from a mother who always made us keep our rooms spotless," said Ray. "Since my divorce, the grocery bill has gone down, but I've spent a whole lot more time at Darby's."

"I hope that will change after this week. Remember to get your vegetables and fruits. Two at each meal is a good rule. Do I need to write that down, or should I get a plaque made for you to hang in your kitchen?"

Ray smiled at his mother. "No, I can remember that. I've got two hands, two feet, two ears. I need to eat two vegetables. Thank you for the cooking lessons this week. I think I can survive now."

"The only problem you have is boiling water. Don't turn on the burner and go do something else, or you'll ruin all your cookware." She couldn't help but frown at the memory of her copper-bottom pot Ray ruined yesterday. "You may have to set the timer."

Ray eagerly changed the subject. "Mom, I think you'll really like your new car. It'll probably remind you of Jessie Bell, with a few more gadgets."

"I think it will help that I've owned a Ford Focus before. I can get your sister to help me understand the computer stuff. Your brother understands all that, but Brad doesn't know how to explain things like Karen does. You could show me a little, but I know you're eager to get back to Georgia. I'm not too old to handle new things."

Sure, Mom. You've got to get used to a new car. I've got a lot more changes than that. I've got to build a new life.

*****

While driving the next thousand miles, Ray did his best to plan his future. He had no choice. General Cleaning was discouraging his coming in early and working late. The project that had consumed his evening hours, devising a Butler Ben that would climb steps, was also cancelled. He now had a new home in a new town, not to mention a different car and a different marital status.

A phrase from the Bible slipped into his thinking, something he'd heard a long time ago: "A peace that passes understanding." He wasn't sure what it meant, but it sounded like God could clear a person's mind when there were too many things to think about at once. Maybe he'd try it.

Travelling down Interstate 81, he prayed for the second time in a week. "God, I've got a lot more to think about than I can handle. Help me straighten things out. Can you give me a peace that is beyond understanding?"

Sometime he wanted to learn how to pray better.

*****

Ray arrived back home at 315 Maple Drive in Horner on Thursday of his vacation week. The first thing he did was rent a small truck. Bill Whitney would be moving in on Saturday, November 14, little more than a week from now.

Boxes lined the walls of every room. Before packing began, Ray made the decision to live out of a suitcase until moving was complete, so that he and Rob Lansing could pack the entire house. This no longer looked like his home.

The kid had been a dynamo. In fifteen hours, Rob had packed the entire house, while consuming four pizzas and seven burgers. Including boxes, bubble wrap, and tape, the total cost had been just under seven hundred dollars, a real bargain compared to a professional moving company.

He had to get out of Horner. It was time for Ray to get on with his new life. He headed out the door to visit Rob Lansing who just happened to be washing his car.

"Hey, Mr. Wright. Glad you're back. When's the moving van coming?"

"Good to see you, Rob." Ray sauntered over to the neighbors' driveway. "I really appreciate the job you did, helping me pack up my house. The money I paid you was certainly well spent."

"Thanks! I haven't spent it yet, but I've been making plans." Rob never looked up, reminding Ray how seriously the kid took the task of shining up his baby-blue vintage sports car.

"Yeah, the house looks deserted. I rented a U-Haul truck for tomorrow and Saturday, thought maybe I could get all these boxes over to Buckner in the next couple days."

"Sounds like a big job," said the lanky teen. "Want any help?"

"Sure, if you think you've got time. I know you've got school tomorrow, but I'll still be working on it Saturday. I'll probably do one load tomorrow and another on Saturday."

"Hey, I'd be glad to help, Mr. Wright! I don't have classes tomorrow, some kind of teachers' training day or something. I could be ready at eight in the morning."

"Great, Rob! Same deal, ten bucks an hour, all the pizza and burgers you want?"

"How about a flat hundred fifty plus food? That'll give me incentive to work harder."

Ray paused for a few seconds. What if they finished the moving in one day? He'd be paying Rob around twenty dollars an hour. Then again,

Ray would have a little time left to do some unpacking.

"Great idea. Rob, it's a deal."

*****

What a Friday! By the end of the day, Ray was as tired as he had ever been. He dreaded tomorrow.

It had been a tough day, but a great day. By nine this evening, every box, every appliance, and every piece of furniture from the house in Horner had made it into the house in Buckner. Ray knew he would be sore tomorrow from all the lifting and carrying (the kid would probably not have an ache anywhere), but it would be worth it.

Piles of boxes were stacked in every room of 107 West Third Street, but at least they were in the house. Ray made sure Rob Lansing helped him get all the heavy furniture in place and the beds put together. Ray would sleep in his own bed tonight.

The only work left at the Horner house was a thorough cleaning, which he would hire done next week. Everything was falling into place. Maybe it had something to do with the prayer he prayed on the way back from New York State, maybe not.

As soon as Ray could find some sheets for the bed, he was going to collapse.

*****

Chapter 7

Ray took a long sip from the styrofoam cup of coffee, part of the breakfast he bought at the Shell station, and set it down on the box next to his recliner. Most of Saturday would be devoted to putting household possessions in their proper place. Now, though, even before finishing his sausage and biscuit and shaving, he began charting a new course.

The words at the top of the yellow pad boldly proclaimed "Building a New Me."

Ray listed several items quickly, finally putting on paper actions that had been running around in his head for many days: Become an outgoing person again, which basically meant to talk more. Buy a rocker for the front porch. Get to know your neighbors. Join a gym. Eat healthy. Replace the shrubbery.

The next items on his list came more slowly. How would he avoid his workaholic tendencies? He added, "Find a hobby" to the list. Next he put down, "Read novels." After several more minutes, Ray wrote, "Learn to pray."

As he predicted, today he ached from the previous day's exertion. In a little while, the list lay on the floor beside the recliner, and Ray was asleep.

*****

Ten minutes ago the restaurant's cashier had called for a manager. Ray wandered around the shopping area at the front of Old Time Vittles. Knowing he only came for one item, he tried to be patient. There were a lot of boxes still to be unpacked in Buckner. Ray couldn't spend all day in Horner.

A thirty-something man with a white shirt and tucked-in tie hurried up to Ray. A gold nametag identified the manager as Art. "Are you the man who wanted to buy a rocker? I apologize for making you wait. Our new cook was having trouble with eggs-over-easy, kept breaking the yolks. Let's go out and take a look at the chairs."

Ray followed the manager out the front door. White rocking chairs were lined up on the porch, as if a dozen people were expected to settle into them at any time.

"I didn't see any price tags. That usually means an item is very expensive."

Art quickly smiled and shook his head. "Classic white rockers like these usually sell for eighty dollars or more. They are certainly worth it, considering they'll last a life time. Our price is sixty. We sold over a hundred last year."

"I'm surprised, actually. They can't be sold as new. I see people rocking in these chairs all the time. That's too much for me to pay for a used rocking chair. Thanks for your time." Ray headed for his car.

Art was stunned. "Sir, wait just a minute. I guess I could sell one for fifty, if you'll promise not to tell all your friends. Where's your pickup?"

Ray replied, "I'm in that white Chevy Malibu over there."

Art shook his head. "There's no way this rocker will fit in your car."

Raymond looked at the rocking chair, then looked at his car. The manager was right.

*****

The driver waved, and the white van pulled away, leaving Ray staring at the front of his new house. It really was a fine porch, looking friendly and inviting with four large white rocking chairs.

Hadn't he gone to buy just one chair? After all, he could only rock in one at a time. Then again, he could only get free delivery with four. Ray had just made a commitment to front porch hospitality.

He glanced down to see a set of eyes, framed by two floppy ears, staring back at him. This cocker spaniel must be the official neighborhood dog.

Like any dog, this one loved to have his chest scratched. After two or three minutes of pleasure, the spaniel walked away, evidently needing to get on with his daily rounds.

Ray settled down in one of his new rockers. He knew boxes inside the house called for his attention, but he had to learn to slow down and enjoy life.

*****

"I've got to get that doorbell fixed," thought Ray. It didn't 'ding dong.' It was more of a 'ding' followed by a few seconds of static.

"Ding scritch-ch-ch." There it was again. He went to the front door and looked out the peep hole. All he could see was the top of a black head of hair. Some kid selling something. Ray didn't need a box of donuts, but if it was magazines, he'd try to buy a subscription.

"Hello. I'm Dale Johnson," said the boy. The black hair was attached to a cute kid, probably nine or ten years old. He had a kind of a half smile stuck between ears big enough for an adult. "Me and my mom live a couple doors down, in the brick house with the green mail box. You've probably met my dog, Sam. He doesn't stay home much when I'm at school."

"Is that the brown cocker spaniel that loves to chase squirrels?" Might as well make small talk. Whatever Dale was selling, he didn't seem to be in a hurry about it. "Your dog comes around every day, religiously." Wrong word. The kid wouldn't understand; he should have said 'regularly.' "Excuse me, Dale, you told me your name, but I didn't tell you mine. I'm Mr. Ray Wright."

Dale said, "Mom would want me to call you Mr. Ray."

"It's okay with me if you just call me Ray. We're neighbors."

The boy thought about that for five or ten seconds, then nodded his head.

"Nice to meet you, Ray." Dale was treating Ray like an old friend, not like a new man in the neighborhood, thirty-seven but probably looking nearly middle-aged. "Are you religious? You said my dog comes by as regular as religion. I'm religious. I'm at church real regular. Me and my mom don't ever miss a Sunday. Can I sit in one of your porch chairs, Ray?"

Dale made himself at home in one of the white rockers. It was way too big for the kid, but Dale quickly had it rocking at a slow, steady pace.

Of course, there was nothing else to do but sit down and talk. The boy just wanted to talk. Good grief, he wasn't even selling anything! The moving truck made it obvious over the past twenty-four hours that someone new was in this house, and Dale Johnson was the first neighbor to come by. Not counting Sam, of course.

"Ray, you're new here. You know anybody yet?" Dale seemed to be a direct kind of guy. What a kid.

"Well, Dale, I know lots of people at my job. I work in Horner, at the General Cleaning plant. I'll meet people on this street eventually. You're the first neighbor to come by and rock."

Dale looked like he felt kind of proud of that fact. They sat silently for a minute or two, rocking almost in rhythm. Sam came along and sat on the first step, waiting patiently for his master.

"Ray, I want you to come to my church tomorrow. I'll introduce you to the neighbors. Most everybody on this street goes to St. John's. Do you know where St. John Community Church is?"

Ray didn't say anything for a minute. Church? He hadn't been to church since he was in high school. Did he have a suit he could still get into? Did he even have a tie anymore? He'd always turned down invitations to churches in recent years. But this was Dale, the kid in the brick house with the green mail box. Dale had chosen Ray as his new friend today.

"Sure, Dale. I've seen the sign for St. John Community Church, just a couple blocks away. I'll be there. Does it start at eleven?"

*****

Sunday morning brought blue skies and pleasant temperatures to Buckner, and no reasons to disappoint a black-haired ten-year-old. Ray was going to church at St. John Community Church just like he'd promised Dale Johnson. Ray had rediscovered a blue suit in his closet that fit surprisingly well, but any ties he might have were evidently visiting their relatives.

This was a good Sunday to walk to church. He went west on Third to Elm, then turned left. When

St. John's came into view, Ray had to smile. It looked like half the congregation wanted to enjoy the weather as long as they could, for dozens stood in little groups outside, obviously lost in relaxed conversation. He was still fifty feet away when two or three people noticed him and soon greeted him with a handshake and a smile. In no time, Ray was brought into one of the conversation circles and began to feel really at ease.

It was a good church service that day. The sanctuary seated maybe a hundred people, not counting the choir. Ray counted seventy-two in attendance, though it was said by somebody that a dozen were gone on a mission trip. Dale spotted Ray halfway through the service and came to sit with him.

Actually, it was not a "good" service. It bordered on "exciting." Though the hymns were traditional, they were sung with enthusiasm. The sermon was relevant and organized. The highlight for Ray was prayer time. Several in the congregation spoke about how God had answered prayers, and several more told little stories about how real God had been to them this week. One man had even felt detained by God from leaving for work on time, only to find somebody had run a red light about the minute he normally would have been going through a certain intersection.

Ray didn't realize until after the service that the forty-something balding pastor was Chuck Burden, whose newspaper column ran in the Horner Herald. Wow! No wonder he sounded like somebody he knew.

*****

Dale's mom, Kathy, dropped by on Sunday afternoon; her son had gone bowling with friends. "Can I sit on your porch? My son says you've got wonderful rocking chairs."

"The chairs would be even more wonderful with cushions, don't you think?" Ray motioned for Kathy to sit.

Kathy looked about thirty-five, with freckles and dimples and shoulder-length dark brown hair. She was not a bit overweight, but had broad shoulders. Something inside made her eyes sparkle.

"I haven't quite figured out how to fit everything into the house," Ray said. "I had about fifty percent more space in the house I owned in Horner. I may have to part with some treasures."

She laughed. "I know what you mean, but my attic is full of treasures I never could part with," she said. "It's a lot easier to add than subtract."

Kathy pointed at various houses in the neighborhood and told Ray who from church lived in them. "See the white house down the street? That belongs to the Wymans. Janet was the lady in the green dress, and Harry had that yellow Big Bird tie. I saw you talking with them before church. Brad and Jenny Smith live across the street in the green house. They've got twin toddlers, Jacob and Sally. Brad's really slim and Jenny's, well, not slim. They sat in front of you. Remember?"

Ray remembered. Little Sally kept turning around and smiling at him. The little boy, Jacob, slept on his daddy's shoulder all through the service.

Kathy and Ray talked for an hour. She had a great sense of humor, and a way of listening that let you know she was really hearing every word. Sam, the cocker spaniel, came by, and Kathy remembered that her son would soon be home. She said her goodbyes and thanked Ray for pleasant conversation.

Over the course of the next two weeks, several of the neighbors came by to visit. Whether or not they got the grand tour of the house, most would linger for lengthy chats on the front porch.

Buckner was beginning to feel like home.

*****

Chapter 8

After three weeks at his new job, Ray had come to a profound conclusion: Management was not easy.

He understood Tom Sullivan's basic goals for Ray as vice-president: Oversee the production of high-quality products, and build an atmosphere in the work place that would foster low turnover.

In past decades, turnover in most companies was not a problem. It was enough for a business to supply a job with competitive pay. Then, ten or fifteen years ago, employees started looking for a job with good benefits. What was the trend now?

Ray had always done well with creative solutions to what future customers would want in vacuum cleaners. Surely he could find an answer to how to retain employees.

He stepped out to the secretary's area. Brenda Darnell could probably help. She'd seen dozens of employees come and go.

"Brenda, I'm trying to figure out why people leave General Cleaning. I'll bet you've got some ideas on that." Ray sat down in one of the two chairs near her desk.

Brenda continued working on the papers in front of her. "I know why some of them leave. They've got folks at home waiting for them. And you only leave because Tom makes you, otherwise you'd be here until dark."

Ray had to laugh. "No, that's not exactly what I mean. Why do people leave this job for another one? Our pay scale is good. We've got good health insurance. Do they want benefits we haven't considered?"

Leaning back in her chair, Brenda took time to think about the question. She tapped her fingers (with her trade mark red finger nail polish) on her desk.

"Let me see. We've had six leave this year, I'm pretty sure. Frank Raleigh and Tina Smith retired. That young guy, Timmy somebody, that stayed just a month, left because he found a job he could do from home. Larry Charles, who had been here forever, said he just didn't feel appreciated. That's four."

Ray said, "Wasn't there somebody here in the office that left?"

"I don't know what Shelly wanted. Maybe a song and dance. She said nobody ever talked to her very much. I thought she liked being left alone, but I guess I was wrong."

They both sat a couple minutes in silence, taxing their memories as to who the sixth former employee had been.

"I know who the other one was," said Brenda. "Clarence the janitor. He's got himself a hot dog stand downtown now. I've been there a couple times. He seems very happy. I think he likes talking with all the folks that come by."

"Everybody here always greeted him when we passed him in the hall."

Brenda once again gave her attention to the papers on her desk. "That's not the same."

*****

In his office, Ray considered the six employees he and Brenda had talked about. There's not much to be done about folks retiring. On the other hand, General Cleaning would benefit if retirement was put off a few years.

Were there any jobs that could be done from home? Should that be an option? Ray could think of many instances in which he had stopped what he was doing to go ask another employee's opinion, or to show them something he was working on. Other times he spent a few extra minutes in the break room, because he could tell that a coworker needed to talk about a project they were working on.

The others that had left might have stayed if there had been more interaction with other workers. General Cleaning had not developed adequate 'family ties' to produce a need in them to stay. Money and benefits could be found at other businesses. The concept of a company being family was new to Ray Wright.

He suddenly realized it had also been something missing in his marriage to Dinah.

People need people. He now knew the cornerstone he'd need in building a better Raymond.

*****

"I'm glad you came by, Ray. Janet and I are sure glad to have all the houses in the neighborhood filled up again. Makes the street feel complete."

Harry Wyman led Ray to the couple's den. Janet lifted her head of pure white hair from the magazine she was reading and smiled warmly. "Hello, Ray. Please sit here in the recliner. Have you gotten lost in our little town yet?"

"Well, I haven't been very far. I really need to see the town. Many people have stopped by to introduce themselves, and I've met some more at church last Sunday. How long have y'all been living here?" Ray settled into the green recliner that matched the one Janet occupied.

"We both grew up in Buckner, Ray," said Harry. "Can I get you some iced tea? We've got sweet or unsweet."

"Thanks, Harry. Unsweet, please."

Ray couldn't help noticing that, though both Harry and Janet were trim and tanned, there was a significant difference in their attire. Janet's dress was a light blue print, while Harry wore a lime green knit shirt and yellow slacks.

"Harry lived on the other side of town, growing up. I lived two doors down and across the street from here, where Brad and Jenny Smith live."

"You mean the green house across from mine?" Ray asked. "You must have been an only child. That's a fairly small house."

"The house is bigger than it appears," replied Janet. "There is actually a full basement, and the upstairs has two finished rooms, not just attic space. My sister and I each had a room upstairs, and my brother Larry had one of the basement rooms."

"I was always envious of that big house," said Harry, returning with three glasses of tea. "I also wished I had siblings."

Janet spoke up, "Ray, I think I can tell from your accent that you are not originally from Georgia. I'd guess Pennsylvania. Am I right?"

With a smile, Ray replied, "That's pretty close. We lived in a small town a little south of Syracuse, New York. My dad was the managing editor of Syracuse's biggest newspaper. There are actually a lot of similarities between here and that part of New York."

Harry said, "You must have relatives there still, I presume. A little bird named Dale told me you work at General Cleaning. I'd have to guess you went to college near here, and just stayed in the area when you found a job. Am I close?"

"Yes, Frank Raleigh hired me right out of Eli Dayton. Dad died ten years ago, but Mom still lives in Etna, the same town where I grew up. I'm the oldest of three kids. My brother and sister and families live near Mom." Ray ventured, "Harry, I don't suppose you play golf?"

Janet began to laugh, while Harry smiled and gave her a puzzled glance.

"Dear, it's your clothes! Ray, that was a wonderful guess, really. I tell Harry all the time that he dresses like a golfer or a used car salesman. He does play golf, but it's the kind referred to as putt-putt." She gave her husband a playful wink.

"Don't be embarrassed at all, Ray. I decided about ten years ago that I was never going to dress like an old man. I want to wear clothes that are lively. God has blessed me with good health, and I'm alive in Christ. These loud clothes make people brave enough to talk to me, and sometimes I get a chance to talk about religion."

Ray thought about his own conservative style of clothing. Is that something that needed a change?

Ray asked, "Who lives in the little brick house in the next block with the blue shutters? I never see more than a room in the back with any lights on."

Harry looked at Janet, then responded, "That's Elsie Crandall's house. She moved here three or four years ago when her sister Doris died. Doris

O'Conner was a faithful church member, but no one can get Elsie to attend. She seems kind of bitter."

"I heard in the grocery store that Elsie blames the doctors for her husband's death a few years ago. That's about all anybody knows. I wish she'd open up a little more," said Janet. "She rarely gets out, and she talks as little as possible when she does."

After a bit of silence, Harry asked, "So, Ray, what did you think of St. John's?"

"I've never been to church much, so I'm no expert. I was impressed by the friendliness of the people. I guess my favorite part was the prayer time. The people seem to be really friendly with God, not just each other. I'm working on improving my praying, so I want to pay close attention to that part of the church service."

Janet smiled. "Keep coming to St. John's, Ray, and I'm sure God will make whatever changes He deems appropriate."

*****

Returning from the Wyman's house, Ray was struck by how unsightly his shrubbery appeared. Does anybody actually like the looks of dead boxwoods?

They had to go, and they had to go soon.

There wasn't more than an hour of daylight left, this Thursday afternoon. He'd attack the bushes tomorrow evening, but today he could formulate a plan.

Ray went to the garage for tools. He grabbed a pair of gloves, a shovel, a pick, and lopping shears. Donning the leather gloves, he grasped the nearest bush with both hands and pulled. It wouldn't budge. He then dug around it with the shovel and pulled a second time. He noted a slight movement.

Would this be a job for a professional?

Ray dug a little more at the base of the shrub with the pick. With a little more digging, this looked like it would work. He quit for the night and put his tools away.

Ray had wanted to start getting more exercise. Joining a gym wasn't working out.

Every time he walked into one of those facilities, with well-muscled men and women lifting huge barbells, he felt like the proverbial 'ninety-eight-pound weakling.' Maybe yard work would be all the exercise he needed for the next few weeks.

*****

Chapter 9

For a week now, the question kept popping into his mind: Why did Elsie Crandall's name sound familiar? He didn't think there had been any Crandalls living near him in Horner. Maybe Brenda would know; it was amazing how many people she knew in the area.

Ray stepped out to the secretary's desk. "Brenda, have you got a minute?"

"I'd better say no. I'll bet you've got something tedious for me to do." She gave him a quick smile. "Just kidding. What can I help you with?"

"One of my new neighbors in Buckner is an elderly lady that lives by herself. I asked a couple down the street from me if they knew her. She really keeps to herself, but they did know her name, Elsie Crandall. Somehow that sounded familiar. Have you ever heard of her?"

Brenda turned from her computer and looked down, deep in thought. After a minute, she ventured, "No, Ray, I don't think so. Now, we had a fellow working here a few years ago, Ralph Crandall. That may be why the name sounds familiar to you. He retired with some kind of sickness, maybe 2010 or 2011."

Ray asked, "Could Elsie have been his wife?"

She turned back to her computer screen. "I can look it up. I think his wife's name would be in his file. Let's see, Carpenter, Chisholm, boy was he a jerk, Crabtree. Here it is."

Brenda electronically leafed through Ralph Crandall's file for a couple minutes, then suddenly stopped.

"Bingo. His wife's name was Elsie O'Conner Crandall. Could that be your neighbor?"

"Definitely. Any idea how Ralph died?"

She looked back at the screen for a minute. "It says complications from heart surgery, 2012."

"Thanks, Brenda. I think I'm starting to remember him. Fairly short, big smile, full head of white hair. That gives me enough to talk about with Elsie when I'm out meeting my neighbors."

"Ray, I think there's something more to meeting your neighbors than that. You don't really have to know a person's history to strike up a conversation."

"You're right. I just get the feeling that meeting Elsie Crandall will give me insight into how to make our company more of a family. Just a feeling."

*****

After two weeks in his new home, Ray had not yet seen downtown Buckner. This afternoon's weather compelled him to take a walk.

The town's east-west streets were numbered, from Seventh Street on the north edge to First at the south. The north-south streets bore the names of trees, except for Main Street, the middle of the five streets.

After going east past Cherry Street, he turned north at the corner of Main Street and Third. After passing Fourth, the next city block was taken up by a bright green and white building proclaiming itself The Grocery Store, and its parking lot. "There's no doubt about what they sell there," Ray said aloud. Continuing up Main, he passed the small brick post office on his right, flanked by a pair of one-story brick duplex apartments.

"Hi, Ray." He turned to see Dale coming up behind him. In his hand were several letters and a magazine. The boy was much shorter than Ray, but had a quick pace.

"Hey, Dale, it's good to see you. I'll bet you've been to the post office. I'm just trying to learn my way around town." Ray added, "I need to go in there soon and get a post office box. I'm still getting my mail at the Horner post office."

Dale said, "Mom likes to send me to the post office so I'll meet more people."

Ray said, "That's a great idea. I'll come back tomorrow and get all that started."

"Better do it in the morning. The post office closes at noon on Saturday."

Now standing at the corner of Sixth Street and Main, a long, one-story home stretched out from the northwest corner of the intersection. The white-frame building evidently arose some time in the middle 1900's, but was well cared for. "Dale, who lives in this big house? They must have a big family."

"That's Annabelle's. It's a restaurant. It's got great food. The parking lot in the back is always crammed with cars. My mom and I go there on special occasions."

Ray had to smile. Annabelle was the name of his brother and sister-in-law's pet dachshund which, like the restaurant, was longer than it was tall.

"Dale, where's Sam today?"

"He's coming. We start out together when I go to the post office, but he always lags behind. Sam has lots of people who need to pet him along the way."

"You're not afraid he'll get lost?"

Dale glanced up at Ray. "He knows his way around, probably better than anybody in town. If he got lost, somebody would call my mom and tell her where to find him."

Ray looked back. Sure enough, Sam was only twenty feet behind them now.

"You need to go into our hardware store," said Dale, looking across Main Street from the restaurant. A red, concrete-block structure took up half the city block. "It's got everything. They've got toys, sporting goods, kitchen stuff, just everything."

"I will, soon," replied Ray. "What other businesses are in town?"

"The only other thing up Main Street is the Baptist Church. They're a lot smaller than our church. If you go east on Sixth, the Methodist Church is on the right, then Jake's Garage on the left. That's it for Buckner."

"Isn't there a gas station?"

"I forgot. The Shell is back down Sixth, at the corner of Elm."

Ray and Dale turned right on Sixth Street, passing the tall brick Buckner Methodist Church. "Do the Methodists have more people attending than the Baptists?" Ray asked Dale.

"A few more, I think. Mom says they have more money. It's better to have more people, like St. John's."

Jake's Garage sported three bays, all in use. Several cars sat at the edge of the parking area, either already repaired or waiting to be fixed. "Take your car there if it ever needs anything. Jake goes to our church, and everybody says he's real good. He's got three kids younger than me."

"Are they the family with two little boys and a little curly-haired girl?"

"That's right, Ray. They always sit in the second pew."

*****

Just follow directions on the back of the package, Mom said. He could do that. In fact, Ray had done quite well cooking vegetables according to the directions on the bag.

So where were the directions on this package of ground chuck for making hamburgers? He looked at the label, but only learned that he had purchased 1.08 pounds of meat at $5.99 per pound. He turned the package over. There were no instructions on the bottom of the package.

Looks like I'll have to rely on my instincts.

Okay, what were the basics in pan frying a hamburger patty?

During his recent cooking lessons Mom had emphasized that he tended to cook on a higher temperature than was necessary. "Have a little patience, son," she said time and again. So he would set the temperature at a medium level.

A hamburger should be flat. In order to pile all Ray wanted on a burger, this was pretty important. Lettuce, a tomato slice, pickles, cheese, jalapenos all needed to stack on the ideal hamburger, so not just any rounded patty would work.

The other imperative, it seemed to Ray, was that a hamburger patty should be round. A hamburger bun was round. All the fast food chains served round burgers.

Ray knew the obvious tool for flattening anything. He found what he was looking for in a big bottom drawer in the kitchen. He covered the rolling pin with plastic, so the meat wouldn't stick to it, and tore off a two-foot length of plastic to put down on the kitchen counter.

He soon had a half-inch thick layer of ground chuck rolled out. Now what? Ray needed four equal round patties. Searching through the cupboard, he spied a small bowl. He inverted the bowl on the layer of beef, cutting out three round patties. The scraps he fashioned into a fourth circle of approximately the same dimensions.

Satisfied, Ray placed the four raw burgers in the large frying pan on the front burner, turning the heat on medium, and started to gather the other items for his sandwich. This was going to be good.

Somehow he doubted Mom formed her hamburger patties this way.

*****

Ray brought his six-foot stepladder to the front of the garage and set it up under the basketball hoop. He didn't even own a basketball, but the hoop just looked wrong without a net hanging from it. The net only set him back a couple bucks but, once installed, it made a huge difference.

Sam padded by, looked at the new basketball net, and wagged his tail. He approved.

*****

Chapter 10

It still felt wrong not to go to work on Saturday. General Cleaning was always deserted on that day, so Ray used to buzz through loads of paperwork easily and had an amazing number of creative ideas. Those days were past. For one thing, the president of the company really wanted Ray to work a reasonable schedule; for another, he promised himself he would build a better Raymond.

He grabbed a bowl out of the kitchen cupboard. Two different cereals vied for his attention. Too early to choose! Ray got both boxes out.

With a full mug of coffee, he planted himself in his usual chair at the kitchen table. He poured a good serving of each cereal into his bowl, then got up to get the milk out of the refrigerator.

Uh-oh. What was left of the milk would be inadequate for the amount of cereal in his bowl. Maybe it would suffice. Lots of folks ate cereal right out of the box.

Note to self: Buy groceries. And don't forget to go to the post office.

*****

"Good morning, Raymond Wright. I'll bet you're here to rent a post office box." The slightly-plump Hispanic lady behind the counter wore the standard blue outfit of the U.S. Postal Service. Her long pony tail draped over her left shoulder, partially obscuring her name badge.

Ray wondered how she knew his name. Wait, he met her at St. John's last Sunday. "You're right, that's why I'm here. Let me see, let me see, your name sounds kind of like mine."

"Renita. That's very good. I know you've met a lot of people."

"You're right. People remember I'm Ray Wright, because I'm the newest resident in town. How long have you been working here, Renita?"

"Twenty-eight years. Does that make me sound old? Ray, don't tell anybody, but my fiftieth birthday is coming up in a few months. This is the only place I've ever worked."

"So," he asked, "what are my choices with post office boxes?"

Renita dug in a drawer for an information sheet. "Now, technically you don't have to rent a box. If you don't, though, you can only get your mail from the counter when the post office is open. The rest of the building is always open, day or night. We don't have anyone at present that doesn't get their mail in a rented box.

"We have two sizes of boxes. The larger size is usually just rented by businesses, but a few people want the larger box because they get a lot of packages. This sheet has the prices for each size, for six months or a year or five years. Which would you like?"

Ray studied the prices for a few seconds. "Renita, I'll pay you for a regular size box, five years." Noting the surprise on her face, he added, "I'm here to stay!"

*****

The first thing Ray noticed, stepping into The Grocery Store, was that it was much smaller than his usual supermarket in Horner. He wanted to buy all he possibly could here, and maybe stop in the store in Horner only every couple weeks.

Maybe he should have made a list. Ray felt a little lost, so even a piece of paper in his hand would help dispel that feeling.

A large lady in jeans and a flowered top tapped Ray on the shoulder. "Good morning, neighbor." Jenny Smith pulled her empty shopping cart parallel to his. "How are you? I love my Saturday morning grocery shopping. Brad keeps the twins so, needless to say, I take my sweet time picking up groceries."

"I'm fine, thanks, Jenny. This is my first time in this store. I don't know where anything is," replied Ray.

"This is your lucky day. If you don't mind dawdling a little, stay right with me, and I'll give you a running commentary on nearly everything in the store."

"Sounds good to me," said Ray.

"Just don't ask me about health foods," Jenny said, and burst out laughing.

*****

It took Ray three trips to the car to unload groceries.

He really didn't mean to buy so much. He just got caught up in the mood of the happy shopper he was with. Jenny introduced him to the produce lady, both workers in the meat department, the manager, both cashiers, and two stock boys.

"Get to know the stock boys well, Ray," she said. "They know all the dirt. They'll tell you if something has been on the shelves forever and a day, what's selling the best, and what's going on sale next week. Ricky and Mel will save you money."

The Grocery Store still used paper sacks! He loved how groceries stayed in place in the old-fashioned bags. Most stores nowadays used plastic bags, and everything just jumbled together.

Besides being a grocery store tour guide, Jenny Smith was a gardener, a canner, and a watercolor artist. It had been a pretty informative morning.

*****

"Ray, I'm Dan Lester, and this is my wife, Maggie. We're your next-door neighbors, in the blue two-story house. We've been out of town a lot lately. It's great to meet you."

Dan Lester was tall, maybe six foot three, with curly black hair. Maggie was a blonde, average height, with a charming smile.

Ray was impressed that people at St. John's were still introducing themselves to him each week after church.

"Nice to meet you. Dan, I've seen you out in the yard the past couple days. I should have come over. You've got a standing invitation to come rock on my front porch any time, even if I'm not home."

Maggie said, "That really looks like a hospitable place, with those four rocking chairs. The lady that used to live there had a couple of straight back chairs and a lot of plants on the porch. All the kids loved Granny Darby. She didn't get outside much in her last few years, except to water her plants."

"I bought the house from her grandson," said Ray. "Stanley said she spent her last year in assisted living, but she really loved this town."

"Have you got relatives in the area?" Dan asked.

"No, my mother and siblings all live in New York State. I went to Eli Dayton, and got a job at General Cleaning when I graduated."

Maggie interjected, "Ray, why don't you join us for Thanksgiving, a week from Thursday? Our daughter is staying at college, at the University of Georgia, for the holiday, so we're inviting some of our friends for the big meal."

Her husband added, "It will help us not think about Debbie's absence. Unless you're going north for the holiday, of course."

"Well, I really didn't have any plans for Thursday," said Ray.

"Then it's settled," Maggie stated firmly. "There will be the two of us, the Wymans, Kathy and Dale, you, and our pastor. That's a perfect fit for our dining room table. And we'll only make you bring a couple cans of cranberry sauce."

*****

Chapter 11

"Welcome, Ray! Here, let me take those cans of cranberry sauce to the kitchen. The neighbors are down here in the den." Dan Lester pointed to the next room down the hall on the right.

Janet Wyman stuck her head out of the den. "Happy Thanksgiving, Ray! We're glad you're here."

He joined Kathy and Dale Johnson and the Wymans in a large paneled room with a dark green sofa, two green upholstered chairs, and a pair of dark brown leather recliners. A platform rocker occupied a distant corner, and it in turn was occupied by Dale Johnson.

Dale called out, "We all just got here, Ray. I hope the preacher gets here soon. I'm getting hungry!" His honest remark caused a wave of laughter around the room. Kathy just shook her head and smiled.

Harry spoke up, "Chuck loves to bake pies. He's bringing a cherry pie and two pumpkin. I suspect he wants them to be fresh out of the oven."

Somewhere in the house, a clock chimed twelve noon, just as the doorbell rang.

Dan called out, "Chuck's here."

Harry smiled. "See what I mean?"

*****

93

Dan was seated at the head of the table, with Maggie to his left. To her left was Harry Wyman, then his wife Janet. Pastor Chuck Burden occupied the chair on the end farthest from the kitchen. Ray found himself seated between Chuck Burden and Dale Johnson, whose mother sat to his left, by Dan Lester.

"Pastor, would you please bless our meal?" spoke Dan.

Chuck smiled. "I defer to you, Dan, as the head of this house. I praise God that our church has more who can pray than just the pastor!" A titter of laughter rose from several of those gathered.

Dan Lester said, "Let's bow and give God thanks." All eight joined hands.

"God our Father, we praise you for all the ways you supply our needs. Thank you for this wonderful Thanksgiving feast, for neighbors and friends, for a wonderful town to live in, and the blessing of a church family that loves you even more than they love one another. We especially thank you for our new neighbor, Ray Wright.

"Lord, take care of our wonderful daughter, Debbie, missing from her place at our holiday meal today. Keep her safe, and help her to be diligent in her studies. May she find many, many ways to be thankful this day.

"Precious Father, draw us ever closer to you. Change us, we pray, for there is so much in us that needs improvement. In the holy name of Jesus we pray, amen."

As hands were unclasped and people raised their heads, Dan added, "And the people said,…"

Dale blurted out, "Let's eat!"

*****

Dishes of sliced turkey, mashed potatoes, whole kernel corn, cranberry sauce, dressing, baby lima beans, and sweet potato soufflé made a circuit around the table. Plates were filled to the very edges.

Ray recognized cornbread dressing, and spooned out a small amount to occupy the only space left on his plate, the very center. He grew up on stuffing, not dressing, but he decided there was so much food on the table that he wouldn't really miss it.

Everyone was involved in happy conversation. Chuck put a small bowl of yellowish liquid down near Ray's plate. What was this? He must have stared at it a little too long, for Dale nudged him and whispered, "Pass the gravy."

Ray whispered back, "Is that what that is? What's the white stuff floating in it?"

"It's gravy. Put it on your cornbread dressing. That's pieces of egg white."

"Oh, okay. Thanks, Dale." He dutifully dumped a scoop of gravy on his cornbread dressing and passed it on to Dale.

Janet Wyman said, "Maggie, I hope Debbie doesn't have to settle for a hamburger for lunch. It's a shame the university couldn't give them a little more time off, so more kids could be with their families for Thanksgiving."

"Debbie explained to us that they are very near the end of the semester. Most kids are studying for finals or writing papers, so they wouldn't have much time to relax anyway. She'll be home soon, and we'll make sure she gets some great food then."

"And vegetables," added Dan. "I think kids on their own avoid vegetables like the plague."

"Please pass the corn," interjected Dale. "I love vegetables."

"Save room for my pies, everybody," said Chuck. "None of them needs to go home with me."

*****

"So how did you end up in Buckner, Ray?"

Kathy decided that Chuck's question was a little blunt. "What he means is, you fit into our community very well. How did we get so blessed?"

Ray put the best spin he could on his recent move. "I guess I needed a little perspective. I wasn't satisfied with my life, especially since my divorce, so I decided to get away from Horner and start over. Maybe God was responsible for how things fell into place, I don't know. Stanley, the grandson of the lady who previously owned the house next door, knew I was looking for a new home, and recommended Buckner as a great place to live."

"Sally loved it here," said Maggie. "She was a great neighbor. You could depend on her bringing pumpkin muffins or sugar cookies to share at least once a month."

Dan added, "Miss Sally really loved children. We've lived next door for the past twenty-four years. Debbie considered Miss Sally an older friend, not somebody's great-grandmother. Good news often made it next door before it got to the ears of Debbie's parents."

Dale patted Ray's arm. "You're not an old lady, but we already love you."

Several around the table chuckled at Dale's remark. Chuck said, "What else are you doing to start over, Ray? We could all use a reboot every now and then."

Ray was quiet for a few seconds. "My job has always been my main focus. The boss at General Cleaning sees that, and wants me to keep my hours reasonable. He's right. I don't want to be a workaholic and die young.

"So I bought some rockers. I really meant to buy one, but ended up with four. I want to enjoy the company of others, and not be so self-absorbed, so y'all come by any time. I'm going to try to get more exercise, too, and join a gym. I also think getting closer to God is something I need as part of the rebuilding process."

"Let me give you fair warning," said Janet. "You need to know that God might make some adjustments you don't anticipate. But don't worry, it'll all be for the best."

*****

After pie, everyone moved to the Lesters' den. Dale took a turkey leg bone outside to Sam, who just happened to be sitting on the front step.

"Harry," said Ray, "your shirt is an interesting shade of tan. I'm used to seeing you in brighter colors."

Harry smiled, and started to speak. Janet beat him to the punch.

"I told him to wear something gravy-colored. Just in case."

Harry laughed. "And I told Janet I'm glad she wore her cranberry-sauce-colored blouse. Just in case."

"Great pies, Chuck," said Dan. "Why did you cut the design of an apple into the crust of the cherry pie? Was it a mix-up with a pie you left at home?" Dan winked at Harry and Janet.

"No," the pastor replied. "I was actually hoping it would resemble a cherry." He added, "And how did you know about the apple pie I have at home?"

Dale rushed in the door, politely stopping next to his mother's chair.

"What is it, son?"

"Ray put up a basketball net! Can I shoot baskets at his house soon?"

"You'll have to ask him, Dale."

Ray spoke up, "Come any time, Dale. You don't have to wait for me to be home."

"Great!" said Dale. "I love basketball, but we don't have a basketball goal at home."

"There's your answer to exercise, Ray," said Chuck. "Shooting baskets is always better with two."

*****

As the guests were preparing to leave, Maggie called out, "Please come to the kitchen and fix yourselves a plate to take with you. There's way too much food left for the two of us."

Ray found himself at the end of the line of those filling a plate. "Could I fix an extra plate for a friend, Maggie?"

"Certainly, Ray. There's still enough for half a dozen friends."

Dan asked, "Did you have a good time? We hoped you would have a chance to get better acquainted with all of us."

"I certainly did. Thank you. I'm looking forward to meeting your daughter some time, too."

Ray filled the two plates and headed out the door.

Arriving home, he put one carryout in the refrigerator. The other he put in a plastic grocery bag, then headed for the next block.

Chapter 12

He rang the doorbell at 210 West Third Street and waited. The porch swing hung unevenly, and could certainly benefit from a new coat of green paint. A mother sparrow chirped from her nest atop one of the corner pillars.

After half a minute, Ray rang the doorbell again, this time twice in succession. He could hear some footsteps at the back of the house, but they weren't getting closer. He decided the doorbell must not be working, and tapped firmly on the glass pane of the front door.

Immediately the steps speeded up and got increasingly louder. A chain was undone, then a key could be heard in the lock. The front door eased open.

Elsie Crandall wore a faded red dress, brown shoes that had seen better days, and narrow reading glasses. Ray guessed her height at halfway between five and six feet. Irritation etched her face.

"The doorbell works. Give me time. I wasn't expecting anybody."

"I didn't mean to be impatient. I'm Raymond Wright. I'm kind of new in the neighborhood, and I'm still trying to meet everybody."

Elsie frowned. "Well, I'm Elsie Crandall. Now you've met me. I don't get out very much, so you probably won't see me around town. What house do you live in?"

"It was Sally Darby's house, if you remember her, 107 West Third, the one with the big front porch. I've got four big rocking chairs out there, feel free to come by any time. They tell me she used the front porch mainly for pot plants."

"I believe I saw her once or twice. I've only been here a little less than four years myself. I believe she brought me a meal the first time she came by." Elsie Crandall snuck a glance at the plastic bag Ray dangled from his right hand.

"I work at General Cleaning in Horton," said Ray. Elsie frowned. "I remember your husband, Ralph, just a little. We worked at different ends of the building."

"You knew Ralph? I sorely miss him. What is your name again?"

"Ray Wright. Elsie, you two must have been quite a pair. I remember he had white hair, just like yours, and you two must have been about the same height. Oh, before I forget, I thought you might like some Thanksgiving dinner. I was invited to eat with my next door neighbors today, and there was a lot of food left. But maybe you had a big Thanksgiving lunch. I don't want to impose on you."

Elsie's face turned dark. "There's nobody to cook for but myself. I just had a can of soup and some crackers. Thank you."

Ray handed the grocery bag to Elsie. "It was nice to meet you. I'd like to come back some time, if you're not busy."

"All I've got is time. Ralph is gone. I'm just hanging on."

She gently closed the door.

*****

Bump, bump, bump, bump.

Reading a novel was different from reading a technical journal. Ray could read a little of a journal, garner a few facts, and then put it down for a while. When he came back, he could pick up where he left off, garner a few more facts, and put it down again. With a novel, there was a plot to keep track of and characters to build an impression of.

A regular bumping was not conducive to reading a novel. Oh, well. He probably wouldn't have finished it on Thanksgiving night anyway.

Ray put a bookmark in his book and went out to the front porch, hoping to find the source of the distracting noise.

"Thanks, Ray. This basketball rim hasn't had a net in a couple years. Come shoot some baskets with me."

Dale dribbled a well-worn basketball in Ray's driveway. He wore tan shorts and a faded brown t-shirt. Sam sat in the grass at the edge of the drive, patiently watching.

His first urge was to tell Dale he was reading a book, but that he was welcome to dribble and shoot as long as he wanted. After all, Ray just barely made his high school basketball team, spending most of three years warming the bench.

"I guess I can play a little while," said Ray. "I never was very good, but I love to play."

The ten-year-old from down the street handled the ball comfortably with either hand. In comparison, Ray looked like a lumbering giant.

"Know how to play horse?" said Dale.

"Sure, Dale. If you make a basket, I've got to make one in the same way, or I get a letter. It takes five letters to spell horse. First one to horse loses."

"You go first. It's your driveway."

Ray dribbled to the line sixteen feet in front of the basket, stopped, and shot. The basketball hit the rim, then the backboard, then the rim, and finally fell through the net. "Is that too long a shot, Dale?"

"Anybody can make a foul shot." Dale lined up at the line and promptly made the shot without even touching the rim.

Ray went back to the line. "But can you make it underhanded?" He ricocheted an underhand toss through the hoop.

Dale stepped to the spot and dribbled about a dozen times, eyes intent on the basket. When he shot, the ball sailed short and to the left.

Ray shot from the left edge of the driveway, barely missing. Dale took the ball to within four feet of the basket. "I'm going to get creative."

The ten-year-old looked at the rim, then the backboard, then the ground, then the backboard again. He slammed the ball into the driveway with two hands, a couple feet in front of him. The basketball shot upwards into the backboard, then looped over the rim and into the basket.

Ray shook his head as he retrieved the basketball. "Wow. Be ready, because I don't have any idea where the ball will go when I try to copy what you just did."

Fifteen minutes later, Sam stood up and padded over to his master. Ray had just barely edged Dale in their game. "It looks like Sam knows I need to go home for supper. Can I leave my ball in your garage, Ray? I don't have a basketball goal at home."

"Sure."

"Thanks. That was fun."

As Dale and Sam were leaving, Ray called out, "I may shoot a little when you're not around. I need some practice."

*****

"Welcome to Buckner Hardware. You missed the Black Friday crowd, they were in and out of here before nine o'clock this morning. What can I do for you?" The slim older man with a long, white moustache and white hair held out his hand to Ray, and they exchanged a firm handshake.

"Good morning. I'm Ray Wright. This is my first time in here. A friend of mine said your store has everything."

Freddy Miller chuckled. "Most everything, I reckon. I'm Freddy Miller, by the way. You must be the fella that moved into the Darby place down on Third."

Surprised, Ray replied, "That's right. I didn't know I was famous. I'm still getting settled in."

"New folks in town are a big deal in Buckner. We treasure our residents, want them to stay forever, and most of them do."

Freddy continued, "I noticed you pulled up your shrubbery. That's a definite improvement. Those bushes have been dead for years. Sally wasn't real mobile in her last year or two here."

"What would you suggest I plant in their place? Maybe I could get something planted before I go back to work Monday."

"We've got some azaleas," said Freddy, "that would be great in front of your porch. You'd have to be patient, though. It would probably be next year before you'd see any blooms. You could plant them about two feet apart, and they'd eventually be a solid wall of flowers in springtime.

"Take a look around while you're here. When you've seen the whole store, pull around to the Main Street side of the building, and you and I will load up everything you need."

This was definitely more than a hardware store. It had a lot in common with the old-time general mercantiles. Buckner Hardware had bulk seed, pet food, farm animal feed, sporting goods, work clothes, magazines, a Christian book rack, motor oil, camping goods, tools, dog houses, and much more.

After twenty minutes, Ray called out to Freddy, "I'm pulling around now. Quite a store you've got here."

*****

By mid-morning on Saturday, the fledgling azaleas were planted, and Ray was pretty worn out. Unfortunately, he doubted he could face preparing much of a lunch.

He wiped his hands on a wadded-up paper towel and pulled his cell phone from his pocket. He scrolled down to Kathy Johnson's number and punched it in.

"Good morning, Ray. You're not Christmas shopping today? You're missing the sales of the year."

"No, Kathy, I've been doing some yard work. I usually do my Christmas shopping in the middle of December, just before I head north to spend the holidays with my folks in upstate New York. Say, is Annabelle's open today?"

"I'm sure they are. Haven't you eaten there yet?"

Ray replied, "No, but today would be a great day. I don't feel like cooking. Can I treat you and Dale to lunch?"

"That would be great. You do know it's a little pricey, don't you?"

"That's what I gathered from what Dale said. I don't mind. Can I pick you up at one?"

"We'll just stop by. It's a good day to walk. See you then."

*****

Chapter 13

Ray saw Kathy and Dale heading up the sidewalk and met them at the door.

Dale offered, "I'll bet you wonder where Sam is. He went to the post office with me this morning, and now he wants to stay in his dog house and rest."

"You're right. I was going to ask. Sam is usually with you. While you're here, Kathy, y'all come in for a minute. I want you to help me figure out my back room." Ray led the way down the central hall to the last room on the left, just past the guest bath.

Stepping through the door, they passed down a narrow passageway, about six feet, into the main part of the room. The nine-foot-square area had book shelves on the two inner walls and a solid wall of windows on the side toward the back of the house.

"I'm just guessing that Sally Darby used this room for reading or sewing. Did you ever see this room when she lived here?"

Kathy said, "Usually we sat in the kitchen to talk."

"She was always baking cookies," Dale interjected.

Kathy chuckled. "She always had treats to give to the children. Sally loved children. One time, though, she was working on a jigsaw puzzle, and invited me back to what she called her 'prayer room.' These shelves were filled to overflowing with books. I remember two or three upholstered chairs like the one you've got, and a small desk of some type, maybe what they call a secretary. She had a card table set up for the puzzle."

"That sounds cozy," said Ray. He wanted to say he would also use this room for prayer, but thought that might make him sound overly pious. He was far from that.

"I need to find a small recliner. I think either of my two recliners from the living room would be too big for this space. A man likes to read in a recliner."

"Moms do, too," said Dale.

*****

"Three?" the hostess asked as they entered Annabelle's.

"Yes. Thank you," Ray replied.

"Can I have a name, please?"

"Raymond."

"You've come at a good time. A lot of our regulars are shopping in Horner or Macon today. Give us just a couple minutes. Feel free to browse in our gift shop."

Dale immediately headed off to a distant corner of the gift shop. Ray didn't know of anything he really wanted to look for, so he followed Kathy as she looked at nearby shelves.

The gift shop was obviously keyed toward attracting impulse buyers. There were lots of signs and plaques, kitchen gadgets, CD's, and books. Various kinds of candy were near the checkout.

"Do you do a lot of cooking, Ray?" Kathy asked.

He shrugged. "I'm learning. While I was married, I guess I took my wife's cooking for granted. She always had breakfast ready when I got up, and supper was on the table when I got home. My part was to wash dishes."

"So, you don't know if you need this convenient vegetable slicer, or that chopping jar we just passed?"

"Right now I'm still at the elementary stage of knife and cutting board. If I ever graduate to kitchen time-savers, I may come back to this gift shop."

She chuckled. "From my experience, I can tell you that not all kitchen gadgets are time-savers."

A cow bell clanged from the far corner. "That's my son," Kathy said. "Dale, put that down and come on. I think our table is almost ready." She whispered to Ray, "They probably had a free table when we arrived, but needed to make us spend time looking at their merchandise."

"Raymond, party of three, your table is ready," called out the hostess.

Kathy smiled at Ray, with arched eyebrows. "See?"

*****

"Ray," said Dale, "I'll bet you didn't grow up in the South."

Kathy interjected, "Now, how would you know that? I think Ray looks very Southern."

"Because, at Thanksgiving, he didn't know what the egg whites in the gravy were." Dale looked across the table at Ray. "Did you?"

"That doesn't mean he's not Southern," said Kathy.

"I grew up in upstate New York. We didn't have egg whites in our gravy. You know, there were other things that were new to me down here. I had never had a tomato sandwich, or a pineapple sandwich, or pimiento cheese. I had seen a pimiento cheese sandwich in a vending machine in Pennsylvania one time, and I remember thinking how strange it looked."

"If you don't know what something is," Kathy said, "it's usually a good idea to pass it up."

"Unless you're a kid," said Dale. "Then they make you eat it anyway."

A short-haired young lady in blue jeans and a button-up red shirt appeared at Ray's elbow. "Hello. I'm Daisy, and I'll be your server this afternoon. Are we just having dessert, or is this a late lunch?"

Ray replied, "It's been a long time since breakfast. We're finally getting to lunch."

Dale quickly added, "Mom says this is lunch and supper for us."

Daisy grinned. "What can I bring y'all to drink?"

All three ordered sweet tea, and Daisy quickly stepped away.

Dale whispered, "Mom, she had blue hair!"

Kathy whispered back, "It's just temporary. She had purple hair last time."

*****

"This smothered chicken is delicious. Kathy, is this kind of dish hard to make at home?"

"No. It's basically boneless chicken breast covered with canned mushroom soup, with a few spices added. Any basic cookbook will have it."

"I'm getting pretty good at following a recipe," said Ray. "If I don't understand some cooking term, I know I can always call Mom. I'll have to try this. Dale, how is your meat loaf?"

"Alright, I guess. It's not as good as my mom's."

"Do you ever get to visit your folks, Ray?" said Kathy.

"I just got back from visiting Mom a couple weeks ago. Dad died a few years back, but I've got a sister and a brother that live near Mom. I try to go a couple times a year."

"I grew up in Pennsylvania, in Wilkes-Barre. Dale and I always go for Christmas, then for a week or two in the summer. Perhaps we could carpool sometime."

Dale asked, "Would there be enough room, Mom? We take a lot of stuff."

"We could cut back on a few things, son, if we knew we were taking another person."

"So, Kathy," said Ray, "this is a long way from Pennsylvania. How did you get to Georgia? Did you get a job down here when you graduated from college, like I did?"

"Almost right. I got married right out of school, and my husband got a job in Horner. I taught in the local school system." Kathy frowned. "But we won't talk about my former husband."

Daisy came by to refill their tea glasses and promised to check on them in a few minutes.

"Mom, are we having dessert?" asked Dale.

"We don't need to spend the money. I've got some cookies at home."

Ray insisted, "No, that's alright. I invited you, and I'm paying. If you can hold it, get dessert."

Dale grinned. "Thanks! A famous guy once said that ice cream cures anything."

"Who?" asked Kathy.

"I don't remember," replied Dale, "I just know he was famous."

*****

He looked around at the little room. An area nine feet square would not hold much furniture. Maybe, instead of a recliner, he should just buy a nice footstool to go with the upholstered chair already in the room. That would leave room for an end table.

He hoped to read a novel every week or two, and slowly fill these shelves.

A box of books sat in a corner, waiting to be unloaded onto the built-in bookshelves. Ray pulled it over in front of the upholstered chair and tried it out as a foot stool. Yes, a foot stool is what he needed.

He could keep a folding chair handy in case he had a visitor. In reality, he envisioned this room as being a private sanctuary, his own little nest. He would read novels here, and newspapers, and ponder great things. This is where he would read the Bible and learn to pray.

Pray? Why did that keep coming up? He had a long list of improvements he wanted to make in 'building a better Raymond.' Maybe it was because it had potential. He'd prayed twice lately, and it had worked both times.

The first time was when he decided to buy this house in Buckner, and Ray asked God if that was okay. God didn't stop him, and it obviously was a great decision. The second time was when he wanted some peace in all that was going on in his life, and things started sorting themselves out. He counted that as a second positive answer to prayer.

He dug in his wallet, looking for the list he had made of how to improve his life, and found the small notepad page neatly folded behind his driver's license. In all, nine items were listed. That was too many.

"Become an outgoing person again." He'd keep that one. "Buy rockers." That was already accomplished, cross it out. "Get to know your neighbors." That was actually part of the first item, so he'd cross that out. "Sign up at a gym for exercise." He had meant to join a gym by now, and still planned to. "Eat healthy." Since there was only one restaurant in Buckner, Ray crossed that out. He cooked most of his own meals, and as long as he did that, he had control over his diet.

"Replace the shrubbery." That could be crossed out. He had planted azaleas where the boxwoods had been, and now they just needed regular watering. It was not really a long-term improvement in his character, but more of a household chore. "Find a hobby." He'd keep that one. "Read novels." Maybe that was a keeper, too, but he would combine it with the previous item. "Learn to pray." That would certainly remain on his list.

Ray turned the list over and made a fresh start. Only four items remained: Become an outgoing person. Join a gym. Find a hobby and read novels. Learn to pray.

Now he had a list he could commit to memory.

*****

Chapter 14

Nine o'clock on the first Saturday in December, and Ray was feeling rather proud of himself. Up since six, he had jumped out of bed, showered and shaved, drove to Horner for a fast-food carryout breakfast, and now a load of laundry was chugging away in the washer. He sat in the den, yellow pad in front of him, ready to map out the rest of the day.

Thump, thump, thump. Sounds like Dale was already out in the driveway, practicing basketball. Ray stepped over to the kitchen window.

No, he was wrong. Today a girl, maybe nineteen or twenty, was practicing hoops at his house. She looked a little familiar, but he decided that he didn't really know her. The girl was tall with braided long blonde hair. She dribbled the ball with ease, and made a good percentage of short to mid-range shots.

He put his athletic shoes on and walked out to the driveway. She looked up, and called out, "Hi there! I'm Debbie Lester from next door. You must be Mr. Wright."

"Good morning, Debbie, pleased to meet you. I guess you must have finished your semester at college."

"Yes, sir. I just got home Thursday night. Thanks for putting a net on the basketball goal. Dale told me you didn't mind us playing."

Ray smiled. "Feel free to come by any time. But call me Ray, Debbie. Dale does. Everybody calls me by my first name."

She tossed him the ball. Ray took a couple dribbles and sank a ten-footer. Debbie corralled the ball as it came through the hoop and quickly dribbled to the foul line, barely missing a jump shot.

After several minutes of alternating shots, she said, "How about a little one-on-one?"

Ray pondered the request. She was obviously a better player than him, though he was four inches taller. Would it bother him to be outplayed by a girl? No, he was beyond that. "Okay. I'll give it a try. I've just played a little horse with Dale."

"You take the ball first. One point baskets. Take it behind the foul line every time. First person to ten."

"Do I get the ball back if I make a shot?"

Debbie shook her head. "No, let's not do 'make it, take it'."

Ray quickly dribbled five feet past the foul line and fired up a jump shot. He missed. Debbie grabbed the rebound, scooted to the foul line, then veered back to the basket for an easy layup.

"I'm stunned," said Ray. "I'd better learn to follow my shot."

"You snooze, you lose," she crowed.

This time Ray dribbled more deliberately, looking for an opportunity to slip by his adversary and get close to the basket. He faked to the left, then went right, leaving her slightly behind as he slipped by to bank in an easy shot.

"That was good. I'll be watching for it next time."

The score stayed close for a few minutes, but Debbie was obviously in better athletic condition. Soon she led by a score of nine to five, and had the ball. Ray had large spots of sweat on his shirt. Debbie looked like she had just arrived.

She dribbled the ball out to twenty feet from the basket. Ray tried to stay close, since she had made a few shots already from this spot.

Debbie faked left, then right. Ray was off balance. She dashed to the left.

Her feet got tangled, and she fell in a heap onto the driveway, putting out her left hand to catch herself. He heard something snap.

Ray saw her pinky finger bent at a sharp angle, bleeding and with bone sticking out.

"Lord, no! Let it be alright!"

Debbie laughed. "Was that a prayer? Hey, I'm not hurt. I just slipped." She got up and dribbled the basketball to the hoop for an easy layup.

Ray screeched, "Debbie, wait a minute! Look at your left hand. Doesn't it hurt?"

She quickly held up her left hand. It looked completely normal, except for a small scratch on her smallest finger.

"I win. I'd better go. Enjoyed it, Ray."

Ray stared with his mouth hanging open. "Are you sure you're okay?"

"Sure. I barely broke a sweat. Next time I'll bring Dale, and we can go two-on-one."

*****

Ray went inside and went directly to the little room at the back of the house. He thought of this as his prayer room.

What did I just see out there?

He was sure of what he saw. Debbie's finger was broken. The bone had been sticking out of the skin, at nearly a ninety-degree angle. He remembered calling out a desperate prayer, "Lord, no! Let it be alright!" And then it was completely healed, leaving only a scratch.

Debbie never knew her finger was broken. God healed it instantly.

He got up and stared out the window. Three different times now, he had prayed a short and simple prayer, and each time God answered. It can't be that easy.

Ray had just started attending church again, after several years away. He was no spiritual giant. And yet God heard his prayers. He had no idea how to pray right. He was just a beginner. Yet he had just seen a miracle with his own two eyes.

It was one thing to know God is almighty, and quite another to see it demonstrated.

*****

"Chuck, this is Ray Wright. I've got a question for you."

Chuck Burden laid his pen down on his office desk and gave his full attention to the parishioner's phone call. "Good to hear from you, Ray. Hope you're doing well this fine day. I'll answer your question as best I can."

"I just saw an out-and-out miracle. There's no other explanation. What I'm wondering about is how the guy's simple prayer got God's attention like that."

"I'll bet the man who prayed had been close to God for a long time. Hebrews eleven six says that without faith, it is impossible to please God. It may have sounded like a simple prayer to you, but there was undoubtedly a lot of history behind it."

Ray knew better. "I don't think so. I know the guy pretty well, and he's what I'd consider a baby Christian."

Chuck unconsciously scratched his head. "Hmm. You know, Jesus did say that if we have the faith of a mustard seed, we can move mountains. How big a miracle did you see, Ray? Could it have been some kind of coincidence?"

"No, this was the real thing. The lady fell, and her finger had a compound fracture. I was close enough to hear the bone snap and see it bleeding and sticking through her skin. The guy blurted out

123

a prayer, and when the lady showed her hand, it was completely healed, with only a scratch."

"Incredible! Wish I could have seen it." Chuck paused for a full ten seconds.

"You know, Ray, don't you think God had you there for a reason? I wonder if those of you who witnessed this miracle might have needed some encouragement in praying. Just hearing your story reminds me, personally, that prayers don't have to be elaborate. It's more important that they be sincere and full of faith in God's ability."

"Maybe so, Chuck. I have been really blessed. Thanks for your time, pastor."

*****

Chapter 15

General Cleaning did its best to contribute to the Christmas spirit by shutting down for two weeks at the end of each year. In addition, employees received four weeks' pay for those two weeks. This year, Friday, December 16, was the last work day until the first Monday in January.

Brenda stuck her head in the company vice-president's office. "Ray, I guess you'll be heading north to spend time with your relatives, won't you?"

He nodded. "I have no choice. My mother would never speak to me again if I didn't show up for Christmas."

She gave him a lopsided grin. "So you're being forced to attend?"

Ray broke out in laughter. "No, no, I love them all. It's sometimes like a circus, with my siblings and their kids, but we love the craziness. What a way to end the year!"

"It's been a wonderful year, except for Frank dying. The company is doing well financially, and, you know, people seem happier here. Ray, you've found some innovative ways to make our employees feel valued. One of the biggest is your daily walk around the plant, chatting with folks."

He paused and looked down at his desk a few seconds. "Brenda, it has helped me a lot, too. I've made a point to learn each employee's name, and get to know them a little bit. I've got some ideas about company get-togethers for next year, but I've got to mull them over a little more.

"So, are you and your husband doing the regular family gatherings for the holidays?"

"You haven't heard?" Brenda broke out a big smile. "Lou and I and our son's family are taking a five-day Caribbean cruise, between Christmas and New Years. I've had to force myself to concentrate on celebrating Christmas first. I've still got presents to buy!"

"Wow, that sounds great! I hope you come back with a great tan. By the way, I hear that they aren't used to red hair down there. You'll make a big impression."

Brenda saw an opening. "By the way, haven't you lost a little weight? You're looking pretty trim."

"I'm down about ten pounds. I didn't know that just putting a net on the basketball goal in my driveway would lead to weight loss. A couple of neighborhood kids come by nearly every day and make me play basketball for half an hour."

*****

Ray stopped at Darby's after work for an early supper. He didn't think he could focus on meal preparation with his Christmas trip to think about.

"Ray, old buddy, I haven't seen you in awhile," said the proprietor. "How's my grandmother's house working out for you?"

"It'll be fine, Stanley. I've still got a few more things to put in place. I'm really enjoying small town life."

Stanley pulled out his order pad. "Is this a sub sandwich day, or do you need a burger?"

"What do you have for rumination?" asked Ray.

Stanley stared at his customer. "Is that like heartburn?"

"No, it means thinking things over. I'm heading to New York State for the holidays, and I'm thinking about how to prepare for the trip. I need food that takes time to eat, something nibbly."

"Got it. Chef's salad. Raspberry lemonade to drink?"

Ray gave Stanley the thumbs up sign, and the proprietor headed for the kitchen.

Let's see, if he left after church on Sunday, he could spend the night in lower Virginia, and then make it to Mom's late Monday. It was nearly eleven hundred miles.

He still needed to buy presents for Karen and her husband, also Brad and his wife. The presents for Mom and his two nieces and two nephews sat in a basket, already bought and wrapped. He wondered whether to buy some small gift for his basketball pals, Dale and Debbie.

Ray usually bought a few snacks for the drive. Hard candy did well. Small chocolate candies kept him awake, as long as he tucked them in his jaw and let them melt slowly instead of chewing them up. He bought coffee whenever he stopped for gas.

A chef's salad appeared at Ray's left elbow. "So, what did you decide to do with the little room at the back of Grandma's house? She called it her prayer room, and it was my favorite. She and I had some long conversations back there."

Ray replied, "One of the neighbors said she read and did jigsaw puzzles in that corner room. It seems like a really private place, somewhere you could disappear with a good novel and not surface for a couple days. I don't have a lot of books yet. Reading is one of my new hobbies."

"What about all those professional magazines you've read in here over the years? Did you just put them in the attic?"

"I only keep a year's worth," Ray responded. "The household electronics field changes so rapidly that news goes out of date in a hurry. Stanley, what kind of books do you read? Got any recommendations?"

"I don't take the time to read. I guess I should. I like the cooking shows on TV. Hey, I've got to get back to the kitchen. Enjoy your salad. I put some jalapenos in, just for you."

Ray got his mind back on the upcoming trip north. Sometimes he'd listen to radio talk shows on the way up. Other times he'd play the alphabet game with road signs as he drove, looking for an "a", then a "b", through the alphabet, just to keep alert. As he recalled, the hardest letter to find on a billboard was "j."

He packed light for these trips, majoring on blue jeans and pullover shirts. Dress slacks and button-up shirts were required for managers at General Cleaning, so he wanted to steer clear of all that on vacation.

His cell phone chimed. Glancing at the display, he could tell it was either Dale or Kathy Johnson. "Hello?"

"Good evening, Ray. This is Kathy. Are you in Horner?"

"Hey, Kathy. I just stopped for a little supper at Darby's. What can I do for you? Is Dale waiting on me to play basketball? "

"My car is having a little trouble with the transmission, and I'm leery about driving it to Pennsylvania Sunday. Jake Ross said it'll take him until Tuesday to get it repaired."

"Boy, that happened at a bad time. Are you going to rent a car?" He knew her job as an elementary school principal must pay fairly well, so the cost shouldn't be a problem.

"Actually, since you're going to New York, I wondered if Dale and I might hitch a ride with you. I know you're probably leaving Sunday after church. That's when we had planned to leave, and we could adjust our return to fit your schedule."

"Well, gee, let me think. I've got presents to take, and I'm sure you do, too."

"Mine are small, Ray. The kids always want money."

"Hmm."

Kathy heard nothing but silence for a half minute.

"Sure, Kathy. I think we can make it work. I'm glad I can help."

"Great! I'll call you tomorrow, and we can work out the details."

After Ray hung up, Stanley stopped by his table. "It's a long, lonely drive to New York, isn't it? You need a traveling companion. Wish I could go with you, but I'm tied to the restaurant."

"Looks like I won't be alone this time. One of my Buckner neighbors just called, and wants to ride as far as Pennsylvania. I wonder if she'll want to drive straight through? It's nearly twenty-four hours driving time for me."

Stanley's eyes perked up. "It's a she?"

*****

This particular Saturday morning was historic. Dale and Ray had outscored Debbie in a game of two-on-

130

one for the first time. Dale was deadly accurate with the basketball from about fifteen feet; Ray just had to lure Debbie far enough away to give Dale an open shot.

Ray sat in one of his front porch rockers after the two younger players left. He was a little tired from the exercise, but he could tell that his stamina was increasing. It seems that God had provided a temporary alternative to getting a gym membership.

He needed to do a little Christmas shopping today, which meant driving into Horner. For the adults on his list, he would buy canisters of some kind. The two women would get kitchen containers, the men he'd buy something for nuts and bolts or small tools.

He wanted to get Dale and Debbie something small, but fun, maybe a toy or sporting goods. Maybe he'd spy something with a quick trip through the big toy store in Horner.

"Good morning, Ray! Let's sit on your porch and rock our way through plans for our trip." Kathy climbed the four steps to the porch and sat in the chair next to Ray's. "Thanks so much for letting us ride with you. I hope your mother doesn't think it's a bigger deal than it actually is."

He looked at his freckled neighbor. "I'm not sure I know what you mean," said Ray.

"You know how mothers are," said Kathy. "You and I are both single, and we're taking this long road trip together. Honestly, Ray, I'm not looking for anybody. Dale and I have gotten used to being a family of two."

"I don't want to offend you," responded Ray, "but it hadn't occurred to me that it might look like a long date. I think of you as part of this incredible group of neighbors I've found in the incredibly friendly town of Buckner."

She smiled slightly, and looked away for a couple of seconds.

"So, are we leaving early tomorrow afternoon? I think I'm nearly packed, and Dale's been ready for three days."

"I'll be ready by the end of today," said Ray. "After church tomorrow, I'll probably want to get my usual Sunday nap."

She said, "I usually drive straight through. Does that suit you?"

Ray thought, *Stopping at a motel might get Mom asking some ridiculous questions.*

"Sure. It'll be nice having a second driver. I think I could sleep in the car alright. But how do you usually drive so far without taking a break for the night?"

"Dale stretches out in the back, and I take an audio book. He can sleep through anything."

"Hey," said Ray, "I like the sound of listening to an audio book. I haven't tried that."

"It'll take two books," she said, "one for the way up and one for the way back. I'll pick one and you pick the other. The hardware store here has a good selection of Christian audio novels. When you're driving, you can listen to the chapters I heard while you were sleeping. And Dale gets his own book, to listen to with earphones."

*****

Amazing, thought Ray. *I stopped in the hardware store for an audio book, and ended up finding all the presents I was going to have to go to Horner for.*

He smiled pleasantly as he walked back to 107 West Third. Glancing back, he saw a friend trailing behind, and waited while Sam caught up.

"So, I hear you're visiting Brad and Jenny Smith while Dale is gone for the holidays."

Sam looked up at Ray and wagged his tail.

"In case I forget to tell you tomorrow, have a merry Christmas, Sam. I left you a little something at the Smith's to open on Christmas morning."

*****

Chapter 16

"Where are we?" Ray let his seat back up and glanced out the windshield. The clock on the dashboard registered a few minutes before noon.

Kathy smiled at him from the driver's seat. "We're finally in Pennsylvania, almost to Chambersburg. We're making good time. How about we stop for lunch soon?"

Ray saw that Dale was sitting up in the back seat with his earphones in. "Great. I always avoid going through Harrisburg during the lunch rush hours. There used to be a great local restaurant in Chambersburg near the interstate."

"You read my mind. Bernie's has a great quiche. Dale always gets the fried egg and mozzarella sandwich. Hey, I caught up to where you were with the audio book. We ought to be able to listen to the last three chapters after lunch, if you don't nap too long."

Ray said, "Thanks for the smooth driving. I guess I slept about three hours. Yeah, if you don't mind driving a half hour after lunch, I'd really appreciate it. That seems to be when I'm the least alert. Just a little nap goes a long ways."

Dale and his mom were great traveling companions. Dale either slept or listened to his own book, and Kathy could chat, talk about deeply personal subjects, or ride in silence. Ray recognized that some travelers were uncomfortable with silence, or made you feel uncomfortable if you didn't speak.

"Kathy, I never have said much about my divorce or marriage. I'll bet you wonder if I was a wife beater or if my wife was some kind of psychopath."

Kathy laughed. "It wasn't information I needed to know. We find plenty of other things to talk about." She paused. "Were you a wife beater?"

They both laughed for a minute. "Actually, I beat my wife up every morning."

Kathy stopped laughing. Silence.

"You did?"

Ray smiled. "I used to get up at five-thirty, and Dinah would get up at six. So, in that sense, I beat her up. And in only that sense." He smiled broadly. Kathy laughed, and looked relieved.

"So, why did you leave her, Ray?" Kathy kept her eyes on the road.

Ray shifted a little in his seat so that he could look at her more directly. "It wasn't me. I was satisfied. One day she just said she was leaving, and had already seen a lawyer."

"Did she give you a reason?"

He shrugged his shoulders. "She just said I wasn't very exciting any more. I have to admit, I was always focused on my work. I spent long hours at General Cleaning, and at night I usually kept my nose stuck in some professional journal, trying to keep up with the industry."

"I guess you could say my Ed didn't find me exciting enough, either. He worked for an insurance company, and ran off with one of the secretaries."

Ray asked, "Were you a workaholic?"

"No, but Ed was. I generally work from seven to four, but he left the house each day at six and didn't get home until around seven each night. He made good money. He spent a lot more time with the people at work than he did with his wife and son.

"Do you have any kids, Ray?"

"No, we never had any children. That's why I act more like a kid around Dale than an adult. I hope that doesn't cause you any problems."

"Dale has lots of adult friends. You can be a kid if you want to. This is our exit coming up."

After taking the exit, they traveled a quarter mile, then Kathy turned the Chevy into the parking area of a small shopping center. They joined a sizeable cluster of cars in front of a storefront with calico curtains and a glass door with a cowbell hanging from it. A small sign over the door declared they had arrived at Bernie's.

Ray turned to look at Dale, who was removing his earphones. "Good morning, Dale. I haven't talked to you in hours. How is today, so far?"

"Good afternoon, Ray. This is a great book I've been listening to. Have you ever read anything by Mark Twain?"

"Sure. Great stuff. I used to read every Mark Twain book I could get hold of. I'm just getting back to reading novels."

Dale said, "Mom says reading takes you to new places. I've been in a little town near the Mississippi River since we started this trip."

They entered the restaurant and sat at a table near the window. A slim, balding waiter soon arrived to take their order.

"Say, I remember you, young man," the waiter said. "Your name is Dan. No, that's not it. Don't tell me. Dave, Don, Dick,…Dale! How are you, Dale? And how are you, Dale's mother with the smile and dimples?"

"We're fine, Ernie," said Kathy, reading the waiter's name badge. "If I gave you a chance, you'd remember my name is Kathy. Good to see you again. Please meet our neighbor, Ray. He's going to drop us off in Wilkes-Barre and head north to around Syracuse."

"Nice to meet you, Ray," said Ernie. "I'll remember you as Ray of Sunshine, so keep smiling. You need to try our pepperoni calzone. Bernie doesn't make it very often."

"Ernie, you wouldn't know, but I was here last December, just before closing, and it was on the menu that day. You're right, it's special. But Kathy recommends quiche, so I'll have that."

The waiter turned to Dale. "Egg and mozzarella on sourdough, with a root beer?"

Dale gave Ernie a big smile and a thumbs up.

"Dale's mom, you want spinach and bacon quiche and black coffee."

Kathy smiled and nodded.

Ernie said, "Dale's neighbor, you should try the other quiche, the Quiche Lorraine. Maybe she'll swap you a taste of her quiche."

"Sounds good," said Ray. "Give me water, and I'll need a coffee to go when we leave."

Ernie nodded and headed for the kitchen.

Ray said, "Kathy, I'm kind of new at cooking, but I figured out how restaurants make their homemade burgers flat. It's simple. They roll the ground beef out with a rolling pin, then cut them with a big cookie cutter. It really works well."

Dale and Kathy stared at Ray.

"What? Are you surprised?" asked Ray.

Dale said, "No, Ray, I think they probably make the burgers like my mom does. She takes some ground beef in her hands, rolls it into a ball, then flattens it between her palms."

Ray looked at Kathy. She smiled and nodded.

Ray just said, "Oh."

*****

After lunch, Kathy drove for twenty minutes, then pulled into a rest area. Ray woke from his nap and got into the drivers seat while Kathy took the other front seat.

"Just stay on I-81 all the way to Wilkes-Barre. My parents live about ten blocks from the interstate. Ready to listen to the rest of the book?"

"Sure," said Ray. "It won't bother your son?"

Kathy looked at Dale in the back seat, lying down and sleeping. "No, he's got his earphones in. He'll sleep through it."

The audio book was nearing a climax. The hero struggled to free himself from ropes tied around his hands and feet, left to die in a ramshackle cabin, far from any homes or regularly-traveled highways. His home church had gathered to pray. They didn't know where he was, only that he was in deadly peril.

In the next-to-last chapter, a hunter passes the deserted cabin and comes inside to spread out his bag lunch. Hearing noise in a closet, he discovers the trussed hero and unties him.

In the final chapter, all loose ends are tied up: The hero is reunited with his family, the criminals are apprehended, and the church celebrates the power of prayer.

Kathy turned to Ray and asked, "Do you believe in prayer?"

He paused before he answered. Should he tell her about the miracle of Debbie's finger being healed?

Ray replied, "I really do. I've seen it work. That being said, I'm not any good at it."

"What do you mean, you're not any good at it? Ray, prayer is just talking to God, and also listening. There's no right way."

He shrugged. "There ought to be a pattern, though, right? Aren't there parts that you always include, and some words you should never say?"

"God wants to hear from your heart," said Kathy. "He's not afraid of your honesty. The part of prayer that pleases God most is your faith. You've got to believe that he'll answer you the best way possible, no matter who you are."

"I've got a lot to learn," said Ray. "Maybe I've been praying right, and didn't even know it."

"The hardest part is trusting that the answer God gives you is the best answer. I prayed and prayed for my husband and our marriage, but it ended in divorce. God's answer was that I was better off without a husband that would cheat on me."

"I guess, in the book we just finished," said Ray, "the criminals wouldn't have thought that getting caught was an answer to prayer. But it was the right thing."

"Ray, our exit is coming up. When you get off the ramp, turn right and then turn left at the second light."

"Don't let me forget to give you the present I got for Dale. Hope he likes it. I got Debbie one, too, but a different color."

In a few minutes, Ray parked his car in the driveway of a white, two-story house.

Kathy said, "When you're helping us carry our bags in, you'll get to meet my parents. Mom will probably try to feed you."

"I'll certainly want to use your rest room. I've still got three hours to go."

Ray noticed a brick church a half block away. "Is that the church your parents attend?"

"You could say it that way," replied Kathy. "My father is the pastor."

A few minutes later, Ray was on the road again. A sixteen-ounce Coke was in the cup holder. A tin of peanut brittle and two ham sandwiches were in the passenger seat.

"Okay, God. Please get me to Mom's in one piece."

*****

Chapter 17

"Raymond, did Karen's computer work for what you needed to do?"

Caroline Wright was hoping her son would volunteer to tell what was so important to order online this morning. If he didn't say, well then, obviously it was a last-minute gift for his mother.

Ray replied, "Sure, Mom. It only took a minute. Please don't ask who it was for. Wednesday is too close to Christmas to be asking that kind of question."

She smiled. His reticence told her all she needed to know. She moved on to a different subject.

She poured herself some coffee and sat down next to Ray at the kitchen table. "Tell me how your cooking is coming along."

"Well, Mom, I haven't burned anything since the last time I was here. I bought a good basic cookbook, *Cooking for Beginners.* I can cook canned or even frozen vegetables. I'm still not very good at rice, so I avoid making it very often."

"How about meats?"

Ray smiled. "The butcher at the grocery store told me what to do with meats. I cook chicken pieces in the oven with a little bit of water in the pan, at three fifty, covered, until I'm sure they're done. I did a beef roast basically the same way, but it took forever. Do the stores ever have beef roasts that are just a pound or a pound and a half?"

"Just buy the regular three or four pound roast," his mom said, "and cut it in smaller pieces after you get it out of the oven and it cools. Freeze all that you can't eat in two meals. Yes, it's certainly not easy to cook just for one."

"Mom, maybe I should invite a neighbor over for a meal every now and then. It would give me a chance to make some larger quantities." Ray hoped his mother wouldn't suggest he find a lady friend to invite for a kind of date.

Instead, she said, "That's an excuse I use for inviting grandchildren over. Of course, I don't need any practice in cooking for a crowd. I had three kids."

Ray asked, "Do you know how to make egg gravy?"

"What in the world is that?"

*****

Ray's family traditionally opened presents on Christmas Eve, then attended Etna United Methodist Church together at six that night. That gave the kids a little time to enjoy their gifts before church, plus all Christmas Day.

Ray sat in the kitchen now, enjoying a Christmas Eve afternoon decaf coffee with his sister.

"It's great to escape the pandemonium," said Karen. Ray's sister looked surprisingly like him, six foot tall with black hair. "Your nieces and nephews are having a wild time with those guns with foam bullets. How did you know Mom would enjoy one, too?"

"It was a bit of a gamble," said Ray. "Either she would love it, and join in playing with her grandkids, or she would just set it aside and wonder if I'd lost my marbles."

"You had her fooled. She thought when you ordered something on my computer, that you were getting a last-minute present for her. What did you order, if you don't mind me asking."

"I've got an elderly neighbor that lives by herself. She's been kind of a recluse. I had a Christmas meal delivered to her yesterday, hoping to make today special for her."

"That was sweet, big brother."

Karen took the opportunity, since no one else had joined them in the kitchen, to steer the conversation to more personal matters. "I haven't had a chance to talk to you one-on-one since the divorce, Ray. I'm sorry it didn't work out. Dinah could be a lot of fun, but at times her energy made me feel inadequate."

"Sometimes I miss having someone else around the house," he responded. "Dinah brought a lot of life into my days. She did have trouble being quiet and still, though. We probably weren't a great match."

Ray's sister asked, "So what are you going to try to change about yourself, if anything?"

"I've put some thought into that, Karen. The biggest change I'm trying to make is to be more outgoing. I've never been all that shy, but I have a tendency to get really focused on projects, especially work. My world can shrink down. It's surprising how enjoyable it has been getting to know my new neighbors since I moved to Buckner."

"It sounds like you're going to be a good neighbor. You know, my husband and I have been married nine years now. I can't remember what it's like being single. What's it like to get back to the dating scene?" Karen asked.

"You're asking the wrong guy. I'm not looking for a new wife. First I want to build a better Raymond."

*****

Over the phone, Kathy and Ray decided to start their return trip to Buckner on Sunday afternoon, even though it was Christmas. They'd miss some of the work week traffic.

"Be sure to find a church to attend up there. God is present in other places, too, not just St. John's. It's unusual for Christmas to be on Sunday, but they will all surely have worship."

He decided on a little country church, reasoning that he wouldn't be expected to dress up as much as in a city church. As he expected, none of the rest of his family chose to attend church, though Mom was a regular at Etna United Methodist.

When he drove up to Ebenezer Baptist Church, his Chevy was the sixth car in the unpaved lot. The front door of the building stood ajar. *I guess that's how they say anyone is welcome,* surmised Ray. He could see a couple of men just inside.

As he entered, a short young man in khakis and a knit shirt extended his hand, saying, "Glad you're here. I'm Reverend Clint."

"I'm glad I'm here, too. I'm Ray Wright. I'm from Georgia, visiting family over the Christmas holidays. It didn't feel right not to be in church because Christmas is on Sunday, so I picked out a place to worship."

"Well, Ray, I'm glad our church was the winner. We'll start in just a couple minutes. We always wait on Miss Mamie."

Ray chose a seat just behind a family of five. The mother and father turned and smiled, introducing themselves as the Browns, and gave him a handshake. The teenage daughter smiled briefly, then resumed her 'I'm-bored-but-my-parents-made-me-come' look. The two little boys stayed busy coloring.

Reverend Clint strode slowly up the aisle, followed by an elegantly-dressed elderly lady in a flowered dress with a black cane. This was obviously Miss Mamie. As soon as Miss Mamie eased herself into the left front pew, Reverend Clint stepped up to the pulpit and began the worship service.

It became obvious that Clint was fairly new at this profession, very unlike Chuck Burden at Ray's home church in Buckner. What Clint lacked in polish, though, he made up for with sincerity. He led the singing with a good voice and a great smile. The sermon on David and Goliath brought out several points that Ray had never considered. He was glad he came.

At the end of the closing hymn, the pastor said, "I think most of you had the chance to meet our visitor before the service. Ray, would you say our closing prayer for us?"

Ray was surprised. He had never been asked to pray in public before. He gave a sheepish grin and rose to his feet.

Lord, help! Get me through this!

"Let's bow for prayer," he started. "God, you've been mighty good about answering my prayers. None of us really deserve anything from you. I ask you to bless this church and its pastor. Help us remember all we've heard today and do it. Amen."

When he opened his eyes, Clint was nodding in approval. He must have done alright.

All sixteen in the congregation stood and eased toward the exit. Ray felt someone tug his shirt sleeve from behind. He turned to see Miss Mamie, probably five foot tall and no more, smiling up at him.

"I'm Mamie O'Conner. Sorry I didn't get to meet you before we started. What's you're last name, Ray? It's great to have a visitor at our little church."

"I'm Raymond Wright, Miss Mamie. Everybody except my mother calls me Ray."

The elderly lady suddenly looked very surprised. "My, my, that's the second time I've heard the name Ray Wright this week. What a coincidence. Where do you live, Ray?"

"I'm from Buckner, Georgia, ma'am. I grew up in Etna, and I'm visiting my mom and relatives for Christmas."

Miss Mamie stared at Ray with her mouth hanging open. Ray had no idea what he said to cause such shock.

"What is it? Have you heard of Buckner?"

After several more seconds, the elderly lady smiled broadly. "Ray Wright, I have a cousin that lives in Buckner. You'll never know how much Elsie appreciated that Christmas meal delivered to her door yesterday."

*****

Ray's choice of a shorter audio book for the return trip to Georgia was fortuitous. Dale felt compelled to describe the Christmas gifts he received in detail. The night-glow flying disk from Ray was one of his favorites.

After stopping for fast food for supper, Ray settled down for a nap while Kathy drove. Dale put in his earplugs to listen to a book. Kathy waited for Ray to nod off before starting the audio book Ray had picked out.

*****

Nearly three hours later, Ray awoke, noting that night had settled in.

"Well, I guess I missed Maryland and West Virginia again. How far into Virginia are we?"

"We just passed Winchester," said Kathy. "I'm amazed that we haven't had to drive in the snow at all on this trip."

"From what I saw of the future forecast, I think we'll be fine the rest of the way. Ready for me to drive?"

She stretched her legs and adjusted herself in the seat. "I'm okay. Let me drive to Staunton, that's a little more than an hour. We'll be needing gas by then."

Ray said, "I did go to church today. It's amazing to me that I hadn't attended church much at all in the last decade, but since the day Dale invited me to St. John's, I haven't missed a Sunday."

"You just didn't know what you were missing."

"You're right," he said. "I thought it was all religion and ritual. Now I'd describe it as relational, both with people and with God."

"So," Kathy said, "tell me about the church you attended today."

"You first. What's it like, going to church with your dad as pastor?"

"It's different, that's for sure. It was just expected that I would sing with the choir, even though I hadn't practiced with them. Every preacher's kid has to support his ministry, you know. And, even as an adult, I felt compelled to be on my best behavior. It was a good worship service, though. Dad's sermons always get to me, even while part of me is focused on cheering for him to do well. I guess that's the power of the Bible."

"Do you remember what the sermon was about? This is a test, to see if you were really paying attention."

"Dad preached on the miracles of the prophet Elisha. Even though it doesn't say Elisha prayed before doing each one, it was evident that his close relationship with God was like living an ongoing prayer."

Ray rubbed his chin. "Wow, that's another aspect of prayer I've got to learn about. Hmm.

"Well, I attended a little church I'd never been to before, a couple miles out of town. The young preacher's message was from the story of David and Goliath. It was good. I'd never noticed Goliath had an armor bearer with him. It was actually two on one."

"And the one was the victor. Just like you and Dale always lose to Debbie at basketball." Kathy couldn't help chuckling at her analogy.

"Kathy, there was an elderly lady at Ebenezer Baptist that actually has a cousin in Buckner. You should have seen her face when I told her where I was from."

She glanced at Ray, then back at the road. "Really? Who is the cousin?"

"Elsie Crandall. I'll have to ask Elsie how she got down here, or how her cousin got up there."

Kathy shook her head. "I hope you can get to know Elsie Crandall. No one else has been able to."

"I guess I may have a little advantage, having known her husband a little from work."

There was also another connection. Ray was working at rebuilding his life. Elsie Crandall needed to rebuild hers just as much as Ray did.

*****

Ray was wide awake, and driving. Kathy and Dale were sound asleep. The CD player continued the drama of the audio book. With only two chapters to go, he decided to finish it. It was good, but not as good as the Christian book they'd heard on the way up. That one had given him more than entertainment. It was food for life.

A little later, Ray ejected the completed book and tuned in to a contemporary Christian radio station. Judging by how long last Sunday's drive took, they should arrive in Buckner around three in the morning. He'd wake Kathy in a couple hours and let her drive the final sixty minutes.

This seemed like a great time to talk to God. He turned down the radio, chuckling to himself. It would be wise not to close his eyes when he prayed this time.

God, teach me to pray. I mean, I don't know what I'm doing, even though it's working.

Aren't I supposed to be more reverent? Other people pray, and I can hear the fear in their voices. I know you're mighty, and you are the judge of all creation, but I know you as my best friend.

I think there are limits to what I should pray, and I've probably passed them, especially when you healed Debbie's finger. Let me know, God, when I ask too much.

I know my prayers aren't long enough. I've got to learn to pray for everyone I'm concerned about, every time. I guess I just thought you knew my concern, so that's why I don't drone on and on with a list. I've got a lot to learn.

I confess, though: It's fun learning to pray. You hear me, even me, among all those millions who pray to you. I just want you to know, I'm ready to learn more.

And, God, do I just say 'amen' when I'm done? Maybe I could be like Kathy said Elisha was, and just keep the line open.

*****

Chapter 18

God came by one day. It caught Ray off guard, but he decided he liked this kind of surprise.

The first week back at General Cleaning in January seemed always to have a problem or two. Employees still had their minds on Christmas, or they were thinking about the credit card bill coming up that included all their holiday purchases. Some had simply gotten out of the routines of the regular work week.

It had been a rough Thursday at work. The Butler Ben vacuum cleaner had recently added a new feature. A red indicator light on the top let the customer know that the rechargeable battery needed to be replaced. A separate note to describe the function of the new indicator light needed to be added to the Portuguese instructions for the load shipping out to Brazil next week, but the company that wrote the original instructions was closed for vacation for two more weeks. Where could they find someone who could write Portuguese? He didn't know anything to do but pray. *Lord, do something, please. Thanks.*

Ray left the problem at work. After supper, he sat in a front porch rocker and sipped a cup of coffee. "What a great place to live," he thought. He looked around at the neighborhood and saw Harry Wyman mowing his front yard. Even cutting grass, Harry was wearing a colorful shirt, a blue and green Hawaiian type.

"Go talk to Harry."

Who said that?

No, it wasn't a voice. It was a thought, just suddenly there in his brain. Ray shrugged. No, Harry's busy. But the idea didn't leave. "Go talk to Harry."

Well, why not? Ray put down his coffee mug and strolled down to the Wyman yard.

Harry smiled big and stopped the mower. "Hey, Ray. Good to see you."

It's funny how conversations ramble sometimes. It's almost like a dog walking around the neighborhood. He finally gets home, but it's the craziest route you can imagine. Ray and Harry talked about many things in just a few minutes.

"Let me show you a picture of my grandkids. Just got it in the mail today. My son and his wife are missionaries, so we don't get to see them very much, but he writes every week." Harry pulled a small envelope out of his pocket and extricated a photo and a letter.

"Wow, Harry, your grandchildren are really cute kids." Ray couldn't help but notice that the letter was in a foreign language.

Harry read from the letter, "This picture was from John's birthday party. By the way, Dad, he opened your present first."

"Ray, I'd let you read the letter," Harry said, "but it's not in English. You don't read Portuguese, do you?" Harry chuckled.

Ray felt his jaw drop open. "Harry? You know Portuguese? How fluent are you?"

"I read and write Portuguese really well, actually. Grandma was a native of Brazil."

Ray had found his translator for the Big Ben shipment.

On his way home later, he said out loud, "God, was that you?" From somewhere within, he felt a strange warmth come over him.

*****

Chuck Burden, like many in his congregation, had gained a few pounds since Thanksgiving. That fact provided the motive for his visit to Ray Wright's house on this particular Thursday evening.

"Pastor, good to see you," said Ray, standing up from his porch rocker. "Grab a seat. What brings you down our street on this fine day in January?"

"Well, I could say that I'm just visiting members of my congregation."

"Good enough," said Ray. "Does that mean you came by to follow up on your last sermon, and quiz me as to the identity of all my neighbors?"

"Good idea, Ray, though I didn't really have in mind to give you a pop quiz." Chuck eased his rocker to a steady rhythm. "In a roundabout way, I've come to talk about Debbie Lester."

Ray was puzzled, but waited for the pastor to say more.

"Debbie kept you and Dale in pretty good shape, playing basketball every day. What will you two do now that she's gone back to college?"

Ray laughed. "Oh, I guess we'll go back to playing a few games of horse every day. It requires less running, but it'll keep our shooting eyes ready for when she comes home again."

Chuck said, "Could I substitute for her? Ray, I've got to get some exercise. My Sunday suits are getting kind of tight. I'm not as good a player as Debbie, but have mercy on me and pencil me into the lineup."

Something about his pastor's earnest plea tickled Ray, and he began to giggle. After a short time Chuck Burden joined the laughter.

Sam came by, looked at the two laughing and rocking, and cocked his head to one side, then the other. He turned and headed back home.

*****

Ray had meant to pay Elsie Crandall a visit when he returned from his Christmas trip north. Other things had come up, and it was Friday, twelve days after Christmas. Now he saw her walking quickly down the street in his direction.

She came up his sidewalk and up to the porch.

"Welcome, Elsie. Please join me. It's a great evening for rocking, though it may get a little cool when the sun goes down."

"Thank you, Raymond. I'll just stay a few minutes." She settled into the rocker two down from him.

"Your cousin said you appreciated the meal I had delivered. I wanted to make sure Christmas was special for you."

"I was certainly surprised when she called and said she met you. Yes, it was very good. And I want to pay you for it."

Ray quickly smiled and shook his head. "Oh, no, that was in the spirit of Christmas."

Elsie quickly responded, "No, I want to repay you. I'm going to make you a good home-cooked meal. I don't often get to invite a guest for supper. I'm hoping you can come tomorrow night at six."

"Yes, ma'am. Thank you, Elsie."

And, with that, she was gone.

*****

The little room at the back of Ray's house had quickly become his second favorite, after the front porch. The furnishings included a comfortable upholstered chair, a small table with a lamp, and a foot stool with a storage compartment. A folding card table and two padded folding chairs leaned against the wall near the door. The built-in book shelves contained only two dozen books at present, most of them reference but would one day be filled with novels Ray had read.

Ray thought back to Chuck's Sunday sermon. He said St. John Church had grown to be the largest church in Buckner by one simple principle: Love your neighbor.

In their early years, members had made it a point to know every single person in their little town. Not only did the St. John congregation know their neighbors, but they also worked at loving and including their neighbors.

Ray could sense by the serious looks on the faces of people as they left church, that the pastor had hit a sensitive nerve. Evidently, there had been less effort in the last couple years to know every single Buckner resident.

He grabbed a pen and pad from the lamp table. How was he doing in meeting his Buckner neighbors?

His block of West Third Street included eight houses, five on his side of the street and three on the south side of the street. The Wymans lived on the corner of Third and Cherry. He had yet to meet the people at 103 West Third, between his house and the Wymans. His other next-door neighbors were Dan and Maggie Lester and Debbie. Then came Dale Johnson and his mother Kathy.

On the other side of the street were three houses. Directly across the street from Ray were Brad and

Jenny Smith and the twins. He had not yet met the residents on either side of the Smiths, although he had waved in greeting several times.

Part of his 'build a better Raymond' plan included continuing to be more outgoing. It was obviously time to meet the rest of his near neighbors.

*****

From somewhere inside, he heard, "Julius, could you get the door, please?"

"Yes, dear."

When the door opened, Ray looked up to a tall, muscular African-American man in khakis and a green knit shirt. "Hello. What can I do for you?"

"I'm Ray Wright. I moved in next door a few months ago, where Sally Darby used to live. I thought it was time that I meet the rest of my neighbors."

The tall man reached out his hand to shake Ray's. "Pleased to meet you, Ray. Julius Ackerman. Just call me Julie. I've seen you playing basketball with your son and daughter. Do you have a wife?"

Ray shook his head. "Those aren't my kids, just some of my young friends from down the street. I'm divorced. We didn't have any kids."

"Julie, invite the man in." A slender lady with shoulder-length black hair appeared at his side.

"Ray, this is my wife, Nancy. Yes, please come in. Nancy, this is Ray Wright, the basketball player from next door." Nancy led them into the room to the right, obviously the den.

As he sat in a dark violet platform rocker, Ray said, "Julius, come shoot some baskets with us some time. You look like you might have played at some time in the past. Nancy, you'd be welcome, too, of course. Debbie Lester has gone back to college, so right now it's only Dale and me. Our pastor has joined us a couple times."

"Where do you go to church, Ray?" Nancy asked.

"I wasn't a churchgoer until I moved here. My young basketball friend, Dale, invited me to St. John Community Church one of the first days I was here, and I've enjoyed it ever since. Y'all please come join us this Sunday."

Nancy and Julius exchanged glances. He said, "We usually look for a black church. Is there one in Buckner?"

Ray rubbed his chin, thinking. "No, there's no all-black church here. We do have quite a few black members in our church."

"Forgive me for saying it, Ray," said Julius, "but I've always found white churches to be rather dull."

"Julius!" Nancy gently tapped her husband on the shoulder.

Ray said, "I guess I've never been to a black church in the South. You may be right. Come give us a try."

*****

What a meal! Elsie had not cooked a great volume of any one menu item, but the variety was tremendous. The baked chicken breasts wrapped in bacon were incredibly tender. There were four vegetables: Purple hull peas, cream corn, pole beans, and broccoli. The mashed potatoes were seasoned with, well, Ray didn't know what, other than it was more than just salt and black pepper.

As Elsie dipped vanilla ice cream out of a pint container, Ray said, "Thank you so much for inviting me over. That was great, Elsie. I'm reminded how much I still have to learn about cooking."

She wore a flowered blue dress, slightly faded, with sandals. She obviously was comfortable with her own looks, for she wore no makeup.

Elsie responded, "I just appreciate someone taking the time to be a neighbor to me. People are very nice in Buckner, don't misunderstand me. Most everyone that lives nearby came to introduce themselves when I first moved in.

"But I was still getting over my husband's unexpected death, and I'm sure I didn't respond with the warmth they probably expected. Ray, it meant a lot to me that you didn't contact me just

163

once, then quit. Your little Christmas gift melted my heart."

They sat silent for a minute, then Ray ventured, "Your husband died. My wife divorced me. I know a little about having to start life over."

"I'm a little old to start over, at seventy. I had decided to just muddle through life, the rest of my years. It gets lonely, though." Elsie stared at her ice cream, her spoon hovering above the frozen dessert..

"You're not too old, neighbor. It's not easy, though. The best thing I've done so far is to respond to a little boy's invitation to St. John Church. They cared for me even before they knew me. I recommend it, Elsie."

"I may try it one day. I'm still trying to forgive God for leaving me a widow.

"Ray, there's a tiny bit of ice cream left. Let me add it to your bowl."

*****

Chapter 19

Ray and Dinah both worked in Horner, but had never run into each other since the divorce. Twice he thought maybe he'd seen her at the other end of a parking lot, but that was it. Now that he'd moved out of town, the chances of encountering her were much slimmer. Yet there she was, on January 10, in the Horner Wal-Mart, heading his way.

"Ray, how are you?" She gave him a big hug, which he appreciated. At thirty-four, she still had the walk and looks of a college student. "I haven't seen you in ages!"

It's been less than a year and a half. But who's counting? He smiled warmly.

He could feel that old affection trying to rekindle in his heart, but the remembered pain kept the wood wet.

"Dinah, you look great. You really do. Are you still teaching at Miller? Of course you are." She nodded vigorously. "I guess you may know that I sold the house. I'm in Buckner now, but still at General Cleaning, of course." He felt like he was babbling. Even if she was his ex-wife, it made his heart flutter to be talking to a gorgeous woman.

"Yep, single and living with Mom." Dinah flashed a big smile. "Me and Doug and Mom are getting along just fine."

Doug? Who was Doug? None of his business.

Dinah saw Ray's facial expression change, and laughed hysterically. "Doug is my mom's cat, silly!"

Ray couldn't help but laugh at himself. He thought, well,...never mind.

Dinah turned serious. "My former husband has changed. You can't hide it, Ray. There's new life inside of you. You *sizzle*, honey. I don't know what it is, but I like it!"

It was hard for him to know how to take the remark. It was a little embarrassing, but also invigorating. They were certainly getting lingering glances from other shoppers going by.

"Look, Ray, Wal-Mart is a wonderful place to meet, but let's get together Saturday. Will you meet me at the Mexican restaurant at six? San Antone at six on Saturday. Alright? Is it a date?"

He just couldn't turn the pretty lady down.

*****

Ray had a lot of trouble concentrating that Tuesday night. His chance meeting with Dinah at the Wal-Mart that afternoon had given him a lot to think about. Was she dating anybody? Surely she hadn't just stayed home every night since the divorce. Was she a church-type person now? They'd never gone to church when they were married, and he knew she didn't go at all when she was growing up. Could he trust her to stay with him if they were to remarry? He hadn't thought about marriage in a long time. It would be really, really nice to have someone to hold, to kiss, to snuggle with, to…well, all that stuff. But, then again, the longer one lives single, the harder it is to share a house with a spouse.

A thought kept pushing its way to the front, and he couldn't ignore it, any more than one could ignore a gorilla in the room: What would Kathy think of Ray having a date with Dinah? Would she be jealous? He had never thought of Kathy as more than a friend, but maybe she would take that as an insult. Did she have feelings for him? Her friendship had become an important part of his life, and he wouldn't want to lose it. Maybe he could hide this date from Kathy. No, friendship requires honesty. He would just have to tell her.

"Lord," he prayed, "work this mess out. It's over my head."

*****

Ray was rocking on his front porch Wednesday when Kathy stopped by. Dale was coming, she said, but the little boy was visiting Dan and Maggie first. "He's so grown up," she said. "People love to have him visit."

"I look forward to my conversations with him, too. He's a straight shooter, and I don't mean just at basketball. And I love his corny jokes." Ray chuckled, thinking about that last 'knock, knock' joke.

Ray decided that he'd better take advantage of this moment with Kathy, before Dale arrived. "You'll never guess who I ran into in Wal-Mart yesterday."

"Oh, let me see. It must be somebody you'd think I wouldn't expect. Was it my ex-husband?" Her dimples came out as she grinned. She knew it was a silly guess.

Boy, she almost hit the nail on the head! "You're actually pretty close. It was *my* ex. And she asked me for a date."

"Wow! That is so cool! You're going, aren't you?" Kathy was so excited, it caught Ray by surprise.

"You think I should?" He paused. "I told her I'd be there."

"Absolutely," she said, in a more serious tone. "Ray, your wife really hurt you when she left. Am I right?" He nodded and tried to smile. "This is your chance to tell her you forgive her. It'll do her a lot of good, but it will do you even more good. Number one, it'll help you understand what it means for God to forgive *you*. And, number two, you need to put the pain of the divorce behind you and move on. You can't do that unless you forgive her."

Ray rocked in silence for a minute. "Kathy, I think Dinah might want to renew our relationship, and I don't know how I feel about that. Got any advice?"

"I sure do. This time, ask God if that's what's right for you. I think you missed that step before."

*****

He stood up and placed the completed novel on the bookshelf. *That was a great book.* Christian novels were definitely what he would read from now on, plus maybe old classics. Too many modern novels depended on sex and murder to keep the reader interested.

Was normal life interesting enough for a novel? His life used to be pretty dull, but since the start of Ray's rebuilding project, exciting events kept popping up.

Maybe that was the change Dinah saw in him. It wasn't more "Ray" shining through, but more of what he was picking up at church shining through.

What would it be like, to pair the effervescent, lively Dinah with the rebuilt Ray?

*****

Chuck and Dale were already shooting baskets when Ray got home Friday evening after work. "I'll be with you in just a minute," he called out, and quickly went in the house to change into shorts and a t-shirt.

By the time Ray emerged from his kitchen door, a third player had joined the other two. "Welcome,

Julius! Couldn't resist the sound of a basketball bouncing, huh?"

"Hello, neighbor! You're right. Don't expect much, though. I haven't played any ball since I got out of high school. It's been fifteen years."

"Friend," said Chuck, "you may be rusty, but you're still tall."

Dale stopped dribbling fifteen feet to the right of the basket and banked a shot into the basket. "Ray, when you're warmed up, it'll be me and Mr. Julius against you and the preacher. He's tallest and I'm shortest, so that ought to be fair."

"Hey, I'm just Julius, Dale. Just another kid in the neighborhood. In fact, you guys can just call me Julie, like my brothers do."

"Are you seven feet tall, Julie?" Chuck took a shot from just outside the foul line, but it clanked off the front of the rim.

"No, no, I'm only six-five. And I'm slower than I used to be."

*****

It was obvious after a few minutes of playing that Chuck and Ray would need to avoid short shots. With Julie near the basket, it was like shooting over a tall tree. Julie blocked more than half their shots.

Dale learned to use Julie's height to great advantage. With the big man between him and the defenders, Dale could loft high shots that they couldn't get close enough to block.

"Ray," whispered Chuck, "maybe if we make a lot of passes back and forth, we can catch Julie out of position."

Ray whispered back, "It's worth a try."

The new strategy seemed to work. Just when Julie was prepared to slap Ray's shot away, the ball was passed to Chuck. Several times it resulted in a basket, but all too often Ray or Chuck missed the open shot.

At the conclusion, Dale and Julie won by two baskets.

"Thanks for a great game, Julie," said Chuck. "I've been trying to lose some weight, and I think I probably lost five pounds today. Wish I could come every day, but pastors have an irregular schedule."

"I'll come when I can," said Julie. "Exercise is a good stress buster. My teaching schedule at Eli Dayton is a pretty heavy load this semester."

Dale spoke up, "Julie, can you and your wife come to church at St. John's this Sunday? Me and Sam can pick you up."

"Surely you don't drive," said their tall neighbor. "I take it Sam is older than you."

"Sam's my cocker spaniel. We'll come by at quarter 'til ten Sunday morning, and walk to Sunday School with y'all, okay?"

Julie boomed out a hearty laugh, and Chuck and Ray joined in.

"Yes, Dale, Nancy and I will be ready. Thank you. See, Ray, I told you we'd try your church sometime."

*****

Dinah had already gotten a booth when Ray arrived at San Antone on Saturday night. She chose a quiet corner, obviously wanting them to be alone.

He slid into the booth, across from his ex-wife. She was blonde and tanned, and obviously still in an aerobics class.

"So good to see you, Ray honey. Have you eaten here lately?"

"No, it's been awhile," he said.

"I come here all the time. It's always good."

The wiry Hispanic waiter came by, and Ray ordered the chicken burrito meal. Dinah ordered the General's Firebrand, but the waiter shook his head. "You don't have it?" He nodded. "Oh, you do have it?" He nodded. "I know it's a little spicy." He nodded, and made motions to indicate his mouth was on fire. "Perfect. I want it." The waiter shrugged his shoulders and wrote it down.

After the meal came, Ray could see the waiter watching surreptitiously, probably to see if Dinah could really handle the spicy food. It didn't seem to faze her at all. She loved it. His chicken burritos were tame in comparison, but equally delicious. They talked about a lot of things, none of it very deep. It was fun to be with Dinah. She laughed easily, and her smile was dazzling.

As they ate dessert, the conversation got a bit more personal.

"Do you miss me, honey? I used to love feeling your arms around me in bed as we went to sleep," she said.

"A little, I guess," he lied. "But I think I snore a little now. It wouldn't be the same. How about you?"

"Actually, Ray, I was married again for a little while, at the end of last year. It hasn't been as long for me." She smiled a kind of half smile.

"Anybody I know? You don't really have to tell me if you don't want to," he said.

"Oh, that's okay. You probably wouldn't know him. I met him at the gym, and thought I was in love. Mike Johansen and I lasted about five weeks." There wasn't a lot of regret in her voice. She just stated facts. "Ray, I'm sorry for leaving you so abruptly. I know it hurt you a lot."

Here was his chance. "Dinah, I totally forgive you for all that. I've turned the page. I don't have any resentment."

She stared at him for a full ten seconds. "Are you sure? Really?"

"Really. Totally forgiven."

She didn't know what to say. The speech she had rehearsed about why she did what she did back then had suddenly become irrelevant.

"Dinah, you told me last Tuesday that you could see new life in me. It got me thinking. I know I'm still a workaholic, recovering. I love my job! I'm not really wilder now than before, though I've really been enjoying rocking on my front porch lately. What was it that made me look different? It must be my new relationship with God that's shining through.

"I've discovered a church where people take God seriously. They sing to God, they worship God, they pray to God, and they even hear from God. Now it's beginning to rub off on me, and it's changing me from the inside out. I've found what I've been looking for."

She stared at her coffee cup. "I wish I could find what I'm looking for," she said, looking a bit tired. "I've been searching my whole life. You know, I think I was happiest when I was with you. I gave up something that I'm never going to be able to get back."

They sat in silence for a minute or two.

"I'm happy for you, Ray. I really am. Look, I've got to be going. It's been great seeing you again. Call me some time.' Dinah gave him a hug and slipped out of the restaurant.

Ray stayed a little longer, slowly sipping his coffee. When it was gone, he prayed a while for Dinah, paid the bill, and left.

He stopped for a moment when he got home, just inside the door. "So what now, God? I sure would like to know your plan. But that's okay, you don't really have to tell me. Thank you for blessing me with four nice rocking chairs. Amen."

Ray went to bed and slept well.

*****

Chapter 20

Ray was one of the first at St. John's to spot them on Sunday, turning the corner of Elm Street and First. The discrepancy in height was almost comical. Dale was still trying to attain five feet, while Julius towered over him, a foot and a half taller. Nancy and Sam followed a few paces behind.

On the other hand, both males wore a white polo shirt and khaki slacks. Nancy looked absolutely stunning in a yellow dress with matching hat.

Before Ray could make his way to his next-door neighbors, Brad and Jenny Smith and the twins had already greeted the Ackermans, and Harry Wyman was introducing them all around.

Julie said, "Nancy, you didn't tell me that Jake Ross and his family attended here."

"You never asked," she answered, as another African-American family headed their way. "I noticed a St. John Community Church bulletin on the counter one day when I was getting my car repaired."

Ray interjected, "You probably ought to know that this church loves to visit outside. Nearly everyone will stay out here chatting until Sunday School begins, then we'll spill out on the lawn again between Sunday School and church."

Nancy said, "It certainly helps visitors feel welcome. I'm already glad we came."

Dale grabbed Nancy's hand. "Come meet Pastor Chuck." She got her husband's attention and brought him along.

*****

After church, Kathy and Dale walked with Nancy back to Third Street. Ray and Julie stayed a little longer at St. John's, chatting with Jake and Thelma Ross and their family, then followed the other three up Elm Street to Third.

As they turned the corner onto Third Street, Julie asked Ray, "Who lives in that green house on the right?"

Ray responded, "That's Elsie Crandall's house. She's been here three or four years, she tells me."

"That front porch swing bothers me. I guess I'm obsessive about order. It hangs a little lower on one side, and needs a coat of paint."

Julius turned up the sidewalk, heading toward Elsie's door.

Surely he's not going to ask her to fix her porch swing, thought Ray. *Lord, get in the middle of this encounter.*

Julie rang the doorbell and waited. "Does the doorbell work?"

"Yes, it works. She takes a little time to get to the door."

Soon they heard the click of the door unlocking. Elsie swung the door open.

"Good morning, Raymond. So good to see you. Who's your friend?" Elsie smiled up at Julie.

"Good morning, Ms. Crandall. I'm Julius Ackerman, Ray's next-door neighbor. I've got a gift for you, if you'll accept it."

Elsie looked at the big man's hands, hanging at his sides, wondering where the present he mentioned might be concealed.

Elsie laughed. "I've just met you, Mr. Ackerman. My mother taught me not to accept gifts from strangers. Do call me Elsie, by the way."

"Thank you, ma'am. I'd prefer you call me Julie. Elsie, I know how to fix your porch swing, to make it hang right. It's just a simple fix, but it will make a world of difference. Would you allow me to take it to my house, down the street, for a few days?"

"I haven't sat in that swing since I've been here. Sure, Julie, I won't miss it. That is certainly kind of you. Raymond, was this your idea?"

He shook his head and held his hands out to his side.

Julie said, "I'll come back in a little while with Ray and the tools I need to take it down."

After Elsie closed the door and the men were headed back down the sidewalk, Julie told Ray,

"The fresh coat of paint I'll put on it will be an added surprise."

*****

The grass was unusually green for mid-January, due to unseasonably warm weather. Still, no lawn mowers or string trimmers, leaf blowers or electric hedge trimmers were ever heard on a Sunday afternoon in Buckner. There seemed to be an unspoken rule that no yard work was to be done on the Sabbath.

He opened the back door and sat down on the top step. Ray's lot covered half an acre, with more lawn in the back than in the front. A six-foot hedge on each side marked the property line. Stanley once mentioned that his grandmother, until her later years, used much of the back yard for garden space. Right now it was an unblemished square patch of green grass, easy to mow.

In Horner, Dinah and Ray used a lawn service to keep the grass and shrubbery trimmed. He quickly learned that all of his neighbors in Buckner did their own lawn work, so Ray bought a push mower, string trimmer, and electric hedge shears to add to the small collection of yard implements he'd acquired when his father died.

What should he do with the yard? He could buy some lawn chairs and a table, but he doubted he'd ever use them. He was really enjoying his front porch rockers.

Maybe he should plant a garden. No, somehow he thought that would be too much to learn. Doing his own cooking and laundry were two educational opportunities already underway.

Surely back yards were not just for mowing.

*****

"Mom, I need some advice."

"Just a minute, Raymond. Let me sit down. This must be an emergency, since you just called me a week ago," responded Caroline Wright.

"It has to do with cooking, Mom. But I'm not starving. I just love your cooking, and want to end up with food that tastes a little like yours."

"Alright," said Ray's mother. "Let's see. You can cook vegetables, you seem to be able to handle several cuts of beef and chicken. Now, I'm not good at seafood. Is that what you need to know?"

"No, that's not it," he said. "I've decided to venture beyond cold cereal for breakfast. What do you suggest?"

"Let's start with eggs. Scrambled is easy, and I can tell you how to easily make hard-boiled eggs. Then you'll need some tips on sausage and bacon. Ray, do you have a toaster?"

"The hardware store here has toasters. I'll get one this week."

Caroline said, "Call me Friday night, and have a pad and pen ready. I'll make sure your sister is not here; I don't need her giggling in the background.

And buy some eggs. You can cook some while I'm giving you instructions over the phone."

After he hung up, Ray decided he was hungry. Annabelle's was just a short walk away.

*****

"Good evening. I'm Daisy, and I'll be serving you tonight." Tonight her hair was orange.

Ray replied, "Nice to see you again, Daisy. I think you were working the only other time I've been in here. Does Annabelle's serve breakfast at night?"

"Yes, sir, any time of the day or night. Do you already have something in mind, or shall I bring you something to drink first while you look at the menu?"

"What are the choices with eggs?" Ray considered himself doing research, in preparation for tomorrow night's cooking lesson.

"You can have them scrambled, sunny-side-up, over easy, or over hard. Every once in a while, someone will ask for hard-boiled or soft-boiled."

"I'll have two eggs sunny-side-up, with sausage and toast. What else might be good?" He hoped to be hungry enough for a wide variety of items, since he was doing basic research.

Daisy replied, "I think you need some hash browns, too. Do you want wheat toast, rye, raisin, or white?"

"Make it raisin toast, please. I'd like decaf coffee to drink."

"I'll have to make some fresh coffee. It'll just take a minute. Can I bring you a glass of water while you're waiting?"

"That'll be great."

Daisy stepped away to the kitchen with Ray's order.

Ray noticed a man about his age, sitting alone a few tables away. He was Ray's size but slightly heavier, wore blue jeans, a white shirt, and a tan pullover sweater. The man was in no hurry to eat his salad, spending much of his time gazing absently out the window.

Nobody should have to eat alone, thought Ray. *Even me.*

Ray gathered up his silverware and napkin and strode to the other table. "Mind if I join you? I'm Ray Wright."

"Not at all. Please do," said the other patron, as he stood to shake hands. "I'm Jimmy Kilpatrick. Folks say a good Irish name like Kilpatrick goes well with my red hair. Where do you work, Ray?"

Ray settled into the chair across from Jimmy. "I work at General Cleaning, in Horner. I moved to Buckner a few months ago. It's a great little town, with lots of friendly people."

He responded with a crooked grin. "Funny you should say that. I'm the pastor of the Methodist

Church here, and I was just thinking about how I might persuade my flock to act a little friendlier, maybe go meet their neighbors.

"Actually, I have two churches, Ray. The other one is on this side of Horner, Westside Church. We run a couple hundred every Sunday over there, with ten and eleven o'clock services. I lead worship here at eight-thirty."

Daisy came by with water for Ray and a chicken pot pie for Jimmy. "I see you found a friend to sit with. Your decaf coffee is just about ready."

"Thank you, Daisy." Ray grinned. "I'm glad you saw I changed seats."

Jimmy moved his nearly-empty salad bowl to the side and centered the pot pie in front of him. "How are you doing at meeting your neighbors, Ray?"

"I know most of them on my block. I've still got to meet the big family that lives at the corner of Cherry and Third, and whoever lives at 104 West Third. Then I'll know my whole block."

Jimmy registered a surprised look. "That's me. I live at 104 West Third. Nice to meet you, neighbor!"

*****

Chapter 21

"Ding scritch-ch-ch." Oh, yeah, he really did need to get that door bell fixed.

"Hi, Ray," said Kathy. "I'm feeling a little nosey. Can I come in?"

"Sure. Great to see you. Dale's not with you?"

Kathy chose the green den recliner near the door. Ray settled into his favorite tan recliner, a few feet away.

"He's home, working on an essay for English. I don't mind leaving him by himself for a little while. I told him where I'd be."

Ray extended the foot rest on his recliner. "Okay, nosey neighbor, what kind of gossip do you need to hear?"

She fidgeted in her seat and didn't speak right away. "I suppose it's really none of my business. On the other hand, I think we're pretty good friends. I care about what happens to you. Of course, some things can be off limits, even between friends. Oh, I don't know, let's talk about something else."

Ray just smiled and waited patiently. It wasn't like Kathy to be at a loss for words.

After an uncomfortable silence, Ray suggested, "I haven't really told you how my date with my ex-wife went. Care to hear about it?"

Kathy smiled and looked relieved. "See, I really am a nosey neighbor. Forgive me."

Ray had to laugh. She was a middle school principal. He was surprised anything could rattle her.

"It's only fair," said Ray. "I told you all about the chance meeting at Wal-Mart. I asked your advice on whether or not I should follow through with the date. It's only fair that I should tell you about the results. It's been nearly a week, and I haven't said a word.

"Hey," said Ray, "I've got some decaf on. Let me get you a cup." He headed over to the kitchen.

"Thank you."

"Do you like chocolate-covered pretzels?" he said. "I picked some up at Annabelle's the other night."

Kathy nodded her head. "That's my favorite."

"Chocolate-covered pretzels?"

"Chocolate anything."

He poured coffee in a mug that proclaimed, "Every day gets better," and poured some pretzels into a small saucer. Ray handed Kathy the mug and the bag of pretzels, and kept the saucer for himself.

"I guess my date with Dinah was a way for her to see if there was any future for us," he said. "She could tell from our chance meeting in Wal-Mart that I'd made some changes."

"Did she seem to regret the divorce? The way you described it sounded rash and heartless."

"She did apologize for the suddenness. I can't blame her, though. I was lost in my work most of the time. I didn't put much effort into the marriage." He shook his head slowly and looked at his feet.

They both took a minute to sip coffee and munch on pretzels.

"And, Kathy, I told her I forgave her completely, like you suggested. I really meant it. It shocked her."

"Now you can start over, Ray. You're different now. So, are you going to see her again?"

"No, it's over. I told her the change she saw in me was from my renewed relationship with God. I don't think she's interested in that subject right now."

"Oh, that's too bad. It's never fun to see a door closed on your life." Kathy raised the coffee mug and drank deeply.

Did he see a smile behind that cup?

*****

January zipped past, and February was down to its last week. Ray, after three and a half months, was getting into a rhythm with his new job at General Cleaning.

Tom Sullivan started his weekly Friday meeting with his vice-president in the usual way. "What's new, Ray?"

Ray Wright pulled a small pad from his shirt pocket. "Looks like we're getting to be more like a family here. Some of the guys from the workshop vacuum section are starting a bowling team. Shirley in electric sweepers is having a baby next month, and they're doing a baby shower for her."

"Sounds good," said Tom. "What about what you said about the uprights last week, maybe some employees coming in early so that the finishing crew wouldn't have to wait to get started?'

"I've reconsidered that," said Ray. "If they came in early, they'd also get to leave early. That might be a distraction. I decided we would do better to leave some uprights partially done each day, so that the finishing crew would have something to start on at the beginning of the day."

Tom leaned forward with both elbows on his desk. "Humor me for a minute, Ray. List for me the kinds of products we make."

Ray looked a little perplexed, but readily obliged. "Let's start at the far end of the plant. We make two kinds of upright household vacuum cleaners, one with replaceable bags and one with water in the canister. We make two models of each. Big Ben comes next, a flat disk vacuum that can clean a home at night or while the homeowner is away for the day. Our electric sweepers are what is often called an electric broom, light and with a smaller dirt capacity. The workshop vacuums come in four sizes, from the mini to the twelve-gallon capacity. Since the year 2000, General Cleaning has manufactured household air purifiers. That's everything."

Tom picked up a pen and tapped a rhythm on his desk. "What's next? Have you thought about new products? We've always depended on you to be our new idea guy. You kept the product development team busy."

"Just a couple crazy ideas. They're more opportunities than solutions. Everybody needs a better way to clean carpeted stairs. Also, there ought to be a way to dust with the power of a vacuum, to get at tiny corners and crevices, computer keyboards, that sort of thing.."

"That last one is an idea from the new kid in the workshop vacuum section."

"Let's see, is his name Randy?" asked Tom. Ray nodded. "Boy, I wonder if we could divert some of his time each week to working on that idea? It sounds like he'd put some energy into it."

"I think we could work it out. We could become the makers of the world's first vacuuming duster. Sounds like a great idea."

Tom said, "Since you stepped into the job of vice-president, you've had limited time to devote to imagining new products. Let's see if Randy could become our next company visionary."

*****

"Raymond, kiss your cold cereal goodbye. I think you can manage to make yourself a hot breakfast every day now. I've got one last piece of cooking advice for you, though."

Raymond looked at his notes from his three breakfast cooking conversations with his mother. He thought he'd have no trouble with sausage or scrambled eggs. The two breakfast casseroles she taught him would be saved for special occasions. Bacon in the microwave would take some practice. The toaster would handle bagels or English muffins or toast. "What more do I need to know, Mom?"

Caroline Wright said, "This applies to all your meals. You need to invite someone to eat with you occasionally. We've talked about this before. When you're always cooking for yourself, it's easy to take shortcuts and slack off, and decide the easy way will be good enough this time.

"When you invite a friend to eat what you've made, you'll be more careful. If they're a true friend, they'll let you know if something is lacking."

"Okay, Mom. I'll be thinking about that. Thanks for all your instructions, and for walking me through making sunny side up eggs while you were on the line."

"I'm always glad to help, son. What are you cooking in the morning?"

"Hard-boiled eggs, a bagel, and brown-and-serve sausage."

"And fruit. Always have fruit. Goodnight, Raymond."

*****

The phone rang, just as Ray completed washing dishes.

"Ray, it's Stanley. How's it going?"

"I'm fine, Stanley. I thought you'd be in bed by now. What can I help you with?"

"I've been to the doctor today," replied Stanley. "He says I've got to get more exercise, or work will kill me. What gym do you go to? I know you talked about signing up with one a few months ago."

Ray frowned. "I never did get started on that. I meant to. Gee, I'm sorry I can't recommend one, friend."

"That's okay. I'll ask some of the customers at breakfast. See you soon. Have a good night."

*****

It was a great novel, but his mind kept wandering. Ray put the book down and looked out on his back lawn.

Something was wrong with his rebuilding project. The call from Stanley last night played over and over in his mind. Was he still building a better Raymond?

He pulled the piece of paper out of his wallet that listed his four goals. First on the list was to become a more outgoing person. That wasn't going like he planned. Instead of talking to people more, he was actually becoming more of a listener.

The second item was a failure. His great plan to join a gym and build some muscles had been replaced by other things. He was not getting more muscular, but slimmer.

The third goal listed was read novels and find a hobby. He had read three novels in four months. Rocking on the front porch couldn't really be called a hobby, could it?

The last item on Ray's list was to learn to pray. God had answered several of his prayers, miraculously at times. Ray still didn't feel like he knew much about prayer. He was just 'flying by the seat of his pants.'

This was not the "better Raymond" he had set out to build. He liked the way his life was going, sure. As far as heading in the direction he'd planned, it looked like his progress was erratic at best.

*****

"Ray, after Chuck and Dale finish schooling us, how about helping me put Miss Elsie's porch swing back up?"

"I'll be glad to, Julie," said Ray.

The score was eight to five. Dale kept finding ways to zip by Ray and Julie for easy baskets, and the pastor had not missed an outside shot all day.

Dale was all alone in the right corner of the basketball court. He lofted up a shot much too long for a ten-year-old. The basketball hit the rim once, twice, then bounced against the backboard and went in.

"Way to go, partner," shouted Chuck.

Julie threw the ball in to Ray, who dribbled midway between Chuck and Dale. When both tried to guard him, he threw the ball high to Julie near the basket, resulting in an easy layup for the tall guy.

"Sorry, guys," said Chuck. "Nine to six. You're starting your comeback too late. We're about to finish the game."

After a half-dozen quick passes back and forth between Dale and Chuck, the pastor found himself with an open ten-foot jump shot. Swish. Game over.

"Way to go, you guys," said Julie. "Dale, when you get to be my height, nobody will be able to stop you."

"Maybe I'll only get to six-three, Julie," said Dale.

"Well, then, there may be one or two that can still stop you. Ray, let's get that porch swing."

The swing looked brand new. The new green paint was exactly the same as the original color.

The chains by which it would hang from the porch ceiling had been replaced by new ones.

Julie parked his Toyota pickup by the street in front of Elsie Crandall's house. The two men carried the swing to the porch, along with a short stepstool. While Ray held the swing, his neighbor hung it from the hooks in the porch ceiling, counting an identical number of chain links on each end.

"You bought me a new swing," said Elsie, coming out her front door. "I never expected that."

"Oh, no, it's the same old swing," said Julie. "I just freshened it up a little."

She shook her head. "That was more than just a little. What do I owe you?"

Julius flashed her a grin. "Not a thing, if you'll use it. You can show your appreciation by sitting out here every now and then."

A mischievous look appeared on the tall man's face. "If you don't use it, I may just sneak down here and strip all the new paint off, so it looks like it used to. Bye now."

*****

Chapter 22

"Randy, Tom and I are intrigued with your idea about a power duster. We're going to give you Monday afternoons away from your regular responsibilities to work on this. We'll bump your pay up five dollars an hour for those four hours each week. Are you willing to give it a shot?"

Ray looked across his clean desk at the bespectacled twenty-two year old. Randy reminded Ray of himself a few years ago, with longish hair, slim build, and eager eyes.

"Yes, sir," said Randy Lewis. "I think this kind of duster is much needed. My wife often asks me to help her dust little corners and hard-to-get-to places, and at those times I wish I had something compact but powerful, with some kind of extension wand."

Ray said, "Let's talk about this a little, and then be prepared to take over this office temporarily every Monday afternoon, starting next week. I'll make sure my stuff is out of your way."

"If you don't mind, Ray, just find me a little room where I can leave things laid out from week to week. It wouldn't need to be much bigger than a closet. I hate to waste company time getting things out and putting them away every week."

Ray considered Randy's suggestion. "I think I can come up with a place. There's an empty office over in Product Development that I used to putter around in. Okay, we're thinking of something that has good suction, for dust that may have been in place for awhile."

Randy added, "And it would need a sharp, pointed nose, to get in small places. I guess the tip would need something soft, maybe a rubber coating."

"Maybe. Battery operated, cordless rechargeable, or with a cord?" Ray asked.

"Hmm. I'm not sure. Each has advantages and disadvantages. I'd better keep an open mind about the power source."

Ray nodded. "I think you're right. And be sure to research what's already on the market. There may be another idea we can improve on. Of course, if some other company already makes this, I think I'd know about it. We're not talking about one of those stubby, hand-held miniature vacuum cleaners.

"One more thing, Randy. Limit your hours on this to Monday afternoons. I don't want you working on it at night, taking time from your wife and little boy. Trust me, the creative process can consume you. Inventing has often led to divorce, my own included. We're determined that General Cleaning be family-friendly."

*****

Two things caught Ray's attention as he pulled into his driveway the last Friday afternoon in February. One, Debbie was sitting on his porch in one of his rockers, with something draped over her right arm. Second, Jessie Bell sat in his garage.

Jessie Bell was Ray's last car, formerly his mom's. The ten-year-old Ford Focus had been there since Ray moved in, because he had just bought Mom's Chevy. He knew he could sell it easily. It had just under eighty thousand miles on it, and ran great. He decided to add it to the 'to do' list, and take it off the 'when I get around to it' list.

Ray exited his Chevy Malibu and walked toward his front porch. It was not unusual for Debbie to come home from college for a weekend, every month or so. Usually she would be playing basketball in his driveway when he pulled up.

"Hi, Ray. I'm home until Monday night. Good to see you."

"Hi, Debbie," said Ray. "What's that on your right arm? Oh, wow, you're wearing a sling!"

"Yeah," she replied. "I was messing around with one of my friends this morning and fell. I put my right hand out to catch my fall, and I guess I sprained my wrist. The infirmary put my arm in a sling and said to go to my family doctor when I got home. Mom's taking me in a few minutes. It's a little sore, but I don't think it's anything serious."

Ray thought back to the time Debbie had fallen on her hand playing basketball, and the miraculous healing he witnessed.

She said, "I just wanted to stop by to tell you how much my girl friends and I have been enjoying the Christmas present you gave me. We toss the glow-in-the-dark disk around after supper two or three times a week." Grinning, she added, "As a fringe benefit, it attracts boys like crazy."

"Wow, that's great. Who would believe I bought it right here in Buckner?" Ray paused. *Should I pray for her?*

Maggie pulled up in front of Ray's house.

"Hey, gotta go. Wish me luck at the doctor's."

Ray blurted out, "Let me pray for you." He took Debbie's left hand, closed his eyes, and said, "Lord, let Debbie's wrist and arm be as good as new. May any tests come out good." Ray wasn't sure what else to say. He just added, "In Jesus' name. Amen."

"Thanks, Ray. See you later. Maybe we can play ball tomorrow."

*****

If he sat in the rocking chair on the west end of the porch, he could see the front yard and porch of every house westward for two blocks. For the months Ray had lived in Buckner, he had never seen anyone from those houses using their front porch.

Until today.

Perhaps Elsie had taken Julie's joking remark at face value, that he would strip all the new paint off her refreshed porch swing if it went unused. She was definitely using her porch swing this evening, and she had company. All he could tell from here was that it was another lady beside her on the swing.

Ray smiled and waved as Jimmy Kilpatrick, the Methodist pastor, pulled out of the parsonage driveway and onto the street. He remembered that Jimmy had planned to visit his parents in Atlanta this weekend. He'd be back late Saturday afternoon.

Maybe this was a good time to try visiting the last neighbor in this block he had not yet met. He got up from his rocker and headed across the street to 110 West Third Street.

Ray knew these folks very casually, from waving at them when they mowed the lawn or pulled out of the driveway in their car. There seemed to be a mother and father, both short and slim with light brown hair, and a daughter with blonde hair that looked to be around six or seven years old.

After ringing the door bell, he stepped back to wait. The door opened almost immediately.

"Would you like a kitten?" the little girl said.

"I don't really need a kitten. But thanks anyway," said Ray. "Do you have a kitten?"

"I have a black one and a yellow one. I like them both, but I can give one away. I don't need them both."

The little girl's mother came hurriedly to the door. "Hello. I'm sorry, I was elbows deep in a sink full of pots and pans. I'm Barbara Simmons."

"I'm Ray Wright, from the brick house across the street. I've been meaning to come introduce myself. I'm glad to meet you, Barbara."

"Won't you have a seat, Ray? I'll go let my husband know we've got company."

Ray sat down in a wicker rocker. The den was decorated in shades of tan and brown. Pictures of their daughter (identified in several places as Elizabeth) were everywhere.

"I'm seven," said Elizabeth. "How old are you?"

Laughing, Ray answered, "I'm thirty-eight. When is your birthday, Elizabeth?"

"I just had my birthday last week. My mom's was yesterday. She's older than you. She's thirty-nine, and my dad's forty. Do you want a Coke?"

Barbara returned just then, her husband a few steps behind. "Why, thank you, Elizabeth. Yes, can I get you something to drink?"

"A Coke would be great, thank you," said Ray.

"I'm Patrick Simmons, Ray. Barbara tells me you moved in across the street. Would that be where The Cookie Lady lived?"

"I bought Sally Darby's house, so I guess that's right. How long have y'all lived here, Patrick?"

"We've been married seventeen years, and I moved in a few months before the wedding, so almost eighteen years. In all those years, we haven't done a very good job of meeting our neighbors."

Barbara returned with Ray's glass of Coke. "We both work in Macon, so with the commute each day, we have all we can do to get the basics done. We're so glad you stopped by."

Ray offered, "It seems, in this town, that the best place to meet people is at St. John Community Church. The ten-year old, across the street from you, invited me when I first moved here. It's been great."

Patrick said, "We've never really had time for church. Sundays are our day to rest up before the busy weekly cycle begins again."

Barbara jumped into the conversation. "Elizabeth goes to Christ United Methodist Church School in Warner Robins and their after-school program until I get off work. She's been learning some things I'm not familiar with, like Noah's Ark and somebody walking on water. I've been telling Patrick that we need to find time to attend church, so we can answer questions she comes up with."

"I can tell you about that, Mommy," said Elizabeth. "Noah built a big boat, called an ark, and loaded all the animals on it, two by two. And Peter was walking on water, because he saw Jesus do it, and he wanted to do it, too."

"Tell you what," said Ray. "You can all walk with me to St. John's this Sunday. I'll come by at quarter to ten. I'll introduce you to some neighbors. They'll make you feel at home right away, just like they did me."

Barbara looked at Patrick. He shrugged his shoulders, then said, "Okay. We can try it at least once. So, Ray, where do you work?"

"I've been at General Cleaning, in Horner, ever since I graduated from Eli Dayton. We make a wide variety of vacuum cleaners, plus a few other things. I was in charge of the Butler Ben until this year, when I got bumped up to management."

Barbara and Patrick started to laugh. Ray looked at them quizzically. He was not quite sure what to say next.

"Ray, we really enjoy our Butler Ben," said Barbara.

"More lately than ever before," added Patrick. "We have a security camera set up at various places in the house. We can access it from our phones or computers when we're at work. Usually all we see on it is our Butler Ben obediently vacuuming while we're away."

"Last month, I glanced at the video one day during my coffee break," said Barbara, "and discovered our kittens had found a new toy. They were riding the vacuum cleaner all over the house. Our security videos have become one of our favorite movies."

Ray shook his head. "Can you think of any features we could add to make Butler Ben better for cats? Maybe a cushioned seat on top?"

*****

Debbie rang his door bell shortly after Ray returned home. He was relieved to see she was no longer wearing a sling, but Debbie was holding her right arm behind her.

"I don't have to wear the sling if I don't want to, Ray. I've got to wear this cast for six weeks," she said, bringing her arm into view. She held out a black marker to him. "Here, you can be the second to sign it. Mom was first."

*****

Chapter 23

Maybe he really didn't know a thing about prayer. Why would God heal Debbie one time and not the other? And what about his project to "build a better Raymond"? His answer to prayers about that were going askew.

Shadows lengthened. Ray needed to leave his rocker and head inside to make a little supper. He stood up and headed for the door, but instead of going in, he decided to go back. The sun was about to go down, and his two rockers on the west end of the porch offered a great view of each evening's sunset. As he turned around, he was surprised to see that a neighbor had come up.

"Good evening, Ray. Can I join you?"

Janet Wyman headed for a rocker on the west end of the porch. "How are you, Ray? What questions about Buckner can I answer for you, now that you've been here for six months?"

"Nice to see you, Janet," he replied with a smile. "What's Harry up to this evening?"

"He decided to cook tonight, and told me to just wander off for an hour or so. So I did. I sat on the porch swing with Elsie Crandall for a while. It's still too early to go home, so here I am.

"I don't even know what Harry's cooking. I just advised him not to burn the house down."

"Maybe he'll cook something out of his grandmother's Brazilian recipes. Is this a special occasion?"

"No," Janet answered. "He surprises me a couple times a year like this. No matter how much I praise what he prepares, it still happens only rarely.

"I'm serious about my earlier question, Ray. Have you got any questions about Buckner? I'm a lifelong resident, you remember."

They rocked in silence for a minute or so. What a beautiful sunset!

Ray began, "It's not a question about Buckner. The first time I visited you and Harry, I mentioned that I was working on improving my praying. Do you remember what you said to me about that?"

She shrugged her shoulders and pondered the question. "I think it was something like, 'God does things in His own style.'"

"I remember your words exactly," he said, "because they sounded a bit mysterious. 'Keep coming to St. John's, Ray, and I'm sure God will make whatever changes He deems appropriate.' God seems to be putting unexpected wrinkles in my progress. My praying is going pretty well, or at least I thought, even though it doesn't always come out in beautiful sentences. God answers my prayers. But I think I've just hit a wall."

Janet chuckled. "Sounds like I said something wiser than my years," she said. "God certainly lets us know He is in control, not us. People want God to help them with their plans. God already has better plans laid out for us. Does that help?"

They rocked in silence a bit more.

"So if I ask for something in my prayers," he asked, "God won't always agree, even if it's for something obviously good?"

"Ray, let me share an experience from early in our marriage." She looked down as she rocked, gathering her thoughts. "Our first child was a miscarriage. We joyfully prepared a nursery for that little girl, only to have something go wrong after seven months. We prayed consistently for that child, but God chose not to save her." Janet cleared her throat several times. When she resumed the story, her voice was much quieter.

"Our second and third pregnancies also ended in miscarriage. Finally, the fourth time around, we were blessed with a healthy, smiling son. Jack is our only child, but no one could ask for a sweeter, more obedient, God-fearing son.

"Jack grew up and married a great girl, and they lived over where Julius and Nancy Ackerman do now. I felt like the world's most blessed woman. But three years ago, everything changed. Jack told us God had called him to the mission field, and they'd be leaving in a few short weeks for Brazil, with our two precious grandsons.

"I cried for days, and cried out to God. How could he take our son, our only son, away from us, after all we suffered before his birth?"

They rocked in silence for a little while. The sun had almost set, and dusk was settling in.

"Janet, that must have been a difficult time. God was taking away your only child." She nodded back at Ray.

"Ray, God had a greater plan. Jack and Wendy have led dozens of people to Christ in the intervening years. We've kept up with our grandsons through letters and videos. They'll be returning from Brazil at the end of this year, to stay. The boys are still young, and they've seen things other kids their age will never be exposed to. It's all good. It certainly wasn't what I wanted God to do. And, you know, I hear the house directly behind us might soon be for sale."

Janet got up to leave. "It's time for me to discover what Harry's cooked for dinner. By the way, I've stopped by to see Elsie a couple times lately. I really enjoy her. I think we can thank you, Ray, for bringing her out of her shell. And she's coming out to swing on her front porch, now that Julie has repaired her swing. That makes it easier for all of us to get to know her."

*****

Janet's conversation this afternoon was only a little helpful. Sometimes God answers prayers with a better solution. What good was a fractured wrist?

As far as 'building a better Raymond,' what was God up to with that? He still needed a hobby, and gym membership. Okay, he had to concede that just living in Buckner had made him a more outgoing person, even if this new person was not exactly how he pictured he would look.

"Ding-scritch-ch-ch."

Ray got up from his recliner and opened the front door. "Well! Stanley, welcome to Buckner. Welcome to the Sally Darby slash Raymond Wright house."

"Hold it a minute, Ray. Let me get a screwdriver out of the car." Stanley walked back to his parked car and quickly returned with a small screwdriver.

"I told my grandmother for ten years I'd see about fixing her doorbell, and just never got around to it." Stanley quickly unscrewed the two small screws holding the doorbell button. "I know exactly why it sounds so funny. See here, Ray? This top wire is loose. I'll tighten it up, and that ought to do it."

Stanley finished the job and pushed the doorbell button. "Ding-dong." Ray reached out and heartily shook his friend's hand. "Stanley, what do I owe you?"

"Fifty bucks," said Stanley.

Ray stared. Silence.

"Just kidding! Boy, you should have seen the look on your face. Can I come in?"

Ray laughed and made a sweeping gesture with his arm, "You are always welcome here, Mr. Fixit. What's up?"

"I just needed a break. I hung a sign on the restaurant door, "Back in the morning," and locked it up. What's a couple hours?"

"Well, let me show you around," said Ray. "You can tell me how Sally's house was set up differently. It might give me some ideas. Hey, you're losing weight, aren't you? You must be getting tired of your own cooking."

"Funny, Ray. You can't get any finer food than Darby's. You know that. No, I signed up at the gym over in your old neighborhood. It's working. I was kind of sore the first week, though."

Ray walked Stanley around the kitchen. "Your kitchen doesn't look right," said Stanley. "Too modern. Grandma's refrigerator was forty years old, and she had a gas stove with only two burners that worked. She had little plaques all over the walls in here. You need something hanging."

Ray countered, "Mom taught me that extras like that just make a place harder to clean. It'll just have to stay plain. Hey, I'll bet Sally Darby didn't own a microwave."

"You're right about that," said Stanley. "Shoot, she didn't even have an electric can opener."

The tour around the house took about fifteen minutes. When they got back to the den, Stanley asked, "What's in the attic? Grandma had it stacked full. It took me two weeks to clean out that part."

"Just some things I don't need, or that I couldn't make fit in the house. I'll probably clean it all out this fall."

"Well, Ray, I like how you've got it all set up. I miss some of the old-fashioned look the place used to have. How do you like the town?"

"It's quiet. I really like it. And this street is especially friendly."

Stanley inched toward the front door. "There's one more thing, buddy. You remember my white car, the one I bought from you ten years ago? The one parked out by the curb?"

"Sure do," said Ray. "Like all my cars, it used to belong to my mother. That would make it twenty years old, right?"

"Exactly. Well, it's starting to show its age, and I see you've still got the car you had, when you bought your mom's most recent car a few months ago. Want to sell it?"

"I would be glad to, Stanley. Let me figure a price."

"Good. Now, don't even bring to mind what a huge bargain I gave you on this house, Ray. Don't even think about it."

"Yes, let's not consider that. The car is ten years old, less than eighty thousand miles, and I know what I paid Mom for it. Hmm."

But Ray did consider the bargain on the house.

"Five thousand sound good, Stanley?"

Stanley Darby pulled his check book out of his pocket and started to write. He wasn't about to let Ray change his mind.

*****

Chapter 24

Bump, bump, bump. Saturday morning. Sounds like Dale had arrived to play basketball.

Ray looked out his kitchen window. Yes, it was Dale, and Julie, too. Sam watched from the grass next to the driveway.

"Good morning, Ray! Time to play a little basketball," said Julie. "We can start with two against one, but I think Debbie's home for the weekend. She'll probably hear us and come out to play."

"I don't think Debbie is in any shape to play basketball right now," said Dale. "Her good arm is in a cast for a few weeks."

"Oh. I hadn't heard. Well, we'll see. She may want to try participating anyway. You know, some people can't stand the sound of a basketball being dribbled without wanting to join in."

Ray volunteered to take on the team of Dale and Julius. He was quicker than Julie, but not as quick as Dale. Ray made a few long shots to start the game, but soon fell behind, unable to cover Dale without allowing Julie near the basket. Dale and Julie soon led by two baskets, eight to six.

"You need some help."

Ray had not noticed Debbie coming up to sit in the grass by the side of the driveway, petting Sam. Debbie had her hair in a pony tail instead of a braid.

She wore jeans today, instead of her usual game attire of shorts and tee shirt.

"Want to play?" said Julie. "You can still pass and dribble with your left hand."

Debbie's face went blank for a minute. "I really hadn't planned to play. I guess I could try. I don't want to slow your game down."

"Are you kidding?" said Ray. "I'm drowning out here!"

It took a minute for Dale and Julie to adjust to the presence of another opponent. In the mean time, Ray made a couple shots to tie the score. Debbie was a pretty decent one-handed passer.

Dale figured out that he didn't have to guard Debbie's right side as well, and concentrated on her left hand. Her passes to Ray got more difficult.

With the score tied at nine, Ray had the ball. Julie hovered over him, daring him to shoot. Not seeing an opening, he passed the ball to Debbie. Ray scurried around the court, trying to get open, while Debbie dribbled and watched. Dale stayed between the other team's two players, hoping to slap away any attempted pass.

Suddenly Debbie faked a pass to Ray, and as Dale leaned, she dribbled toward the basket. She scooped the ball toward the backboard with her left hand, and it ricocheted in.

"Wow! Nice move, kid!" exclaimed Julie.

"You guys thought I was a cripple, didn't you?"

Dale said, "Just don't tell people you beat us with one hand tied behind your back."

"Debbie, I broke my good arm in high school," said Julie, "and I learned to shoot with my other hand. After Dale and I beat you two in this next game, I'll give you a few pointers on shooting left-handed. But I want to wait until after we win."

*****

It was time. Really, it was past time. All these months, the whole neighborhood had been playing basketball with Dale's basketball. And everyone knew that the hardware store in town had everything.

"Hey there, Ray. What can I do for you?"

Ray was pleased that everyone in Buckner seemed to know his name. Buckner was a special place.

Ray replied, "I'll bet you've got a good basketball, Freddy. We've been playing a lot of basketball in my driveway lately, and the ball Dale brought a while back is looking pretty worn. I need to buy him a new one."

"Step over to the last aisle. We've got some especially made for outdoor hoops."

Ray followed Freddie Miller to the far wall shelf. "I see you've got some backyard croquet sets. I haven't played croquet in years."

Freddy said, "I don't think people in Buckner play much croquet. I've had those two sets for a couple years. Ray, I'll sell you one for half price."

"Thanks. Why not? I've got a big back yard that would be perfect for croquet. Surely I can get somebody in the neighborhood interested."

He looked over the basketballs, ranging in price from eight dollars to twenty. It would make sense to get the best he could, so it would last.

"How many of you are playing?" asked Freddy. "Sometimes it's nice to have more than one ball, when several are just shooting and not playing a game."

Ray ended up with two basketballs, an audio book, and a croquet set.

*****

Janet's advice made sense. God had a better perspective and a bigger plan than he or anyone else. Prayers could be answered in ways that God knew were best, but not look like good answers to the average person.

He took out the little list of his goals from his wallet and laid it on the foot stool in front of him. He wanted to become a more outgoing person. He needed a hobby. He needed to join a gym for exercise. He wanted to learn to pray.

A month ago, he gave himself a bad grade on his progress related to this list. Maybe he wasn't doing that bad, after all.

Even though he was listening more in conversations than previously, Ray was talking with others more readily. That was probably a better outcome than his original intent. An outgoing person didn't necessarily monopolize a conversation.

He had wanted a hobby. Well, he was not only reading books, but also listening to audio books.

His idea of joining a gym for exercise wasn't working out. On the other hand, Ray played basketball now several times a week. Judging by the amount he sweated, that was certainly exercise. Playing basketball with the neighbors was a hobby, too.

Was he praying any better? Sometimes God answered his prayers, but sometimes the things Ray prayed for just didn't happen. Debbie's arm came to mind. He had prayed she would be healed instantly, like the time her broken finger was healed. Why had God not answered that prayer? What did he do wrong?

Maybe God had a better plan. With Julie's help, Debbie could now shoot a little with her left hand, even though it would be several weeks before she could shoot a basketball with her right hand. Could that be God's answer to Ray's prayer?

He got up from his chair and looked out the back window. God was taking over Ray's goals. He decided he was alright with that. Maybe building a better Raymond was more in God's job description than his own.

*****

Kathy called late Saturday afternoon. "Care to join me for grilled hamburgers tonight? You can come early enough to see how I patty them out, along with my secret seasoning."

"I'll be glad to," Ray responded. "Let me bring some ice cream for dessert. What time do y'all eat?"

"Come about five. Dale won't be with us tonight. Brad and Jenny are letting Dale watch the kids, while they go to a movie. I promised the Smiths I'd be at home, in case Dale needed anything. This is his first time babysitting the twins without Brad or Jenny being in the house."

It almost sounded like a date. No, Kathy was a friend and neighbor. This would be fun.

In the hour he still had before heading to Kathy's house, Ray took his new croquet set to the back yard and set up the wire hoops in the figure-eight pattern he remembered from his childhood. He made a quick practice round through the course.

On the other side of the hedge, he heard Julie call out, "Nancy, do you hear that? I'll bet our neighbor is playing croquet. Let's go bother him." Within two minutes, the Ackermans had come around the back edge of the hedge between the houses.

"Say, we haven't played croquet in years" said Julie. "I still recognize the sound, though. Ray, can we join you for a game?"

"Glad to have you two," said Ray. "First, though, I need to know how you play. Are you going to spend your time trying to put your ball through hoops, or is one of you the type that concentrates on knocking his competitor's ball all over the court?"

"Perhaps we'll let you discover that as we go along," said Nancy.

Ray soon found out that Nancy was the more cutthroat player. The normally-gentle lady next door found great joy in sending other wooden balls flying.

"We heard the ruckus over here from our back porch," said Dan Lester. "Can the three of us play?"

"There are six mallets in the set, just enough. Join us!" said Ray.

About the time Ray needed to leave to go to Kathy's for supper, one more head poked around the corner of his house. "Oh, sorry, Ray. I didn't mean to intrude. I just stopped by to say hello. Just got back from Atlanta."

"Good to see you, Jimmy," said Ray. "Do y'all know Jimmy Kilpatrick, from across the street?"

The Ackermans and Lesters stopped playing long enough to introduce themselves.

"Listen, folks," said Ray. "I've got an appointment at five. Please stay. I didn't know this neighborhood needed a croquet set. Jimmy, would you take my place?" Ray handed the Methodist pastor his mallet.

*****

Chapter 25

Ray wore jeans, like Kathy suggested. By coincidence, both wore black knit shirts.

Kathy made cooking look easy. The entire time she was preparing and grilling the hamburgers, putting together the salad, and making deviled eggs, she carried on an easy conversation with Ray.

They sat down to eat at about six o'clock. "I'll say the blessing, Ray, if you don't mind. It's my privilege, as the host."

He nodded his assent, feeling relieved.

"Dear God, our heavenly father and best friend, thank you for this meal and the many ways you supply our needs. We praise you for a good church, good neighbors, and good friends. May we always seek to pass your blessings on to others, not just keep them for ourselves. In the precious name of Jesus we pray, amen."

"I see you like jalapeno slices on your hamburgers, too," said Ray. "Life ought to be a little spicy."

"I thought Dinah divorced you because you weren't spicy enough," responded Kathy. "Oh, that's right, she said you'd changed."

"I've always liked food a little spicy. I've got more spice in my spiritual life now. That's what she noticed, I think."

Kathy nodded. "Feel free to add jalapeno slices to your salad. Ray, you said you'd never made deviled eggs. Think you could do it now, after watching me?"

Ray pondered the question for a few seconds. "I might not add all the spices you did. They might be good enough for me with just mayonnaise and sweet pickles added to the egg yolks. But I remember all the basics. See, you've improved my life."

After the meal, Kathy dipped some of the cherry vanilla ice cream Ray brought into bowls. "Let's take these into the living room to eat, where the chairs are more comfortable. Don't tell Dale, though. I don't let him bring food into the living room."

Ray found a comfortable platform rocker to sit in. Kathy settled into a recliner nearby.

She said, "You and Dale both seem to love platform rockers. Y'all have many things in common."

When they'd finished and placed their bowls on the coffee table, she reached over and took Ray's hand. "I've been wanting to talk to you about something personal, Ray. Is that okay? I consider you a good friend."

A flood of emotions rushed his brain. This was getting serious.

Seeing that she was unnerving him, Kathy released his hand and drew hers back to her lap.

"You likely remember me telling you, Ray, that Dale's father left me for one of his secretaries. I was not about to let him have any visiting rights. None whatsoever. His morals would be a bad influence on my son, even if he only saw him every other weekend. He didn't fight me on that. All I asked was that he buy an annuity that Dale could access when he got out of college, to help him get a good start in his career. He owed me that much. It'll be worth two hundred thousand dollars at that time.

"So Dale's father will never be part of his life. That's why I'm so glad to belong to such a good church. The men in St. John's have been great examples to my son of how a Christian man should live his life."

Ray nodded. "They really are fine men. All the people at our church have impressed me. I want to grow in my Christian life to be like the folks at St. John's."

"There's something else, Ray. When Dale was born, I had several problems. The biggest concern was a small tumor in my abdomen that had to be removed right after the delivery. It turned out to be benign, praise the Lord. Ever since then, especially since the divorce, I've wondered who would raise Dale if something happened to me."

"Kathy, I hope you don't think about that much. Dale is already ten, and you told me you just had a great annual checkup."

She was silent for a full minute. She took Ray's hand again.

"Ray, would you agree to become Dale's legal guardian if I were to die? I would never want him to be given back to his birth father. Nothing will probably happen to me any time in the near future. I really am healthy. It would just make me feel more content if I had this taken care of."

Silence enveloped the room for the next several minutes. Ray rocked in the platform rocker while Kathy closed her eyes and stretched out in the recliner.

Ray finally spoke up. "I propose we make a compact, with two things that will most likely not happen. You know that all my relatives live in New York, right? If I were to die unexpectedly, who would handle my estate? It would be a major problem for my sister or brother to have to handle all the details at a distance.

"Would you be the executor of my estate? If you'll do that, I'll do you the similar favor of signing up as Dale's legal guardian."

She said, "If you die before I do."

He said, "And if Dale is not an adult when you die."

Kathy and Ray stared intently at each other. She got up from her recliner; he got out of the platform rocker.

"Let's shake on it," Kathy offered.

"Good idea." Ray extended his hand, and they shared a firm handshake.

They both sat down.

Ray asked, "So why me, Kathy? I've never raised any kids, and I'd be a single parent. How about the Wymans, or maybe Dan and Maggie? Don't get me wrong. I'm not trying to back out of our agreement. I just wonder why you chose me for such an important responsibility."

She brought the recliner back to the upright position and folded her hands in her lap. "Ray, whether or not you realize it, you've given me a good picture of the man you used to be. You admit Dinah had reason to divorce you, even though most women would have given you a little more slack.

"The old Ray was a workaholic. He was focused on himself and the project most important to him. He didn't spend time with his wife or anyone else. I would never have considered asking the old Raymond Wright to help raise my son.

"You are not that man anymore. The Ray I know is outgoing, and intent on getting to know his neighbors. The Ray Wright we have now in Buckner listens to other people, and makes an effort to include and be kind to all people.

"You're a man who treats women fairly. You've got female friends of all ages, like Elsie, Janet, me, and Debbie, not thinking of them as prizes or something to be pursued, but friends.

"Ray Wright works hard, but he's not a workaholic anymore. You've got time to play with kids. You operate a wide-open front porch, with four available rockers.

"What I love most about you is you've made God a high priority in your life. You never miss attending Sunday morning worship. You are a praying man, and seeking to know God better.

"For all of these reasons, I would be proud for you to take over raising my son, if the need ever arose. I trust you with my most valuable possession."

Ray rocked in silence for a couple minutes, giving his red face time to cool down.

He ventured, "Same here."

"What?" Kathy looked puzzled. "What do you mean?"

Ray said, "That last thing you said is why I asked you to be the executor of my estate. I trust you with my most valuable possessions."

Kathy's doorbell rang, and both of them went to the door.

"Just bringing Dale home, Kathy," said Brad Smith. "He did a great job with the kids tonight. The twins are both asleep."

"Mom, I read seven books to them. I think they slept through most of the last one."

"Good job, son! Ray and I had a nice neighborly supper. He left you a little ice cream, didn't you, Ray?"

Ray forced a smile. "I sure did, Dale."

He had been hoping to take the last of the ice cream home.

*****

Chapter 26

What a great day! It was Sunday, and Ray had arrived.

He suspected as much, but Kathy confirmed last night that he had done it: He had built a better Raymond. Just as she said, he was not the man he used to be.

It was true that God deserved the greatest part of the credit. Ray had set goals and God had made adjustments. Instead of joining a gym, Ray was playing basketball. Instead of monopolizing conversations, Ray was a good listener. He had a hobby, actually two, basketball and reading. And he could pray, though God sometimes answered in better ways than Ray asked.

So, now that the offering plate had passed, Ray and the rest of the congregation at St. John Community Church were eager to hear Chuck Burden's sermon. Sometimes Chuck was funny, sometimes extremely serious, but always they could tell he'd spent a lot of time with God, preparing a message that would go straight to their hearts.

"Today I'm going to let you listen in on a sermon that's meant for me," started Chuck. "If it applies to you, great. If not, well, just be thankful.

"My father taught me to pray when I was very young. Many of you learned the same simple prayer I did. If so, join me as I recite it."

As the pastor began the prayer, more than half the congregation joined in. "Now I lay me down to sleep. I pray the Lord my soul to keep. If I should die before I wake, I pray the Lord my soul to take. Amen."

Chuck continued, "I think it was my mother that taught me the Lord's Prayer, when I was ten. Let's pray that together now."

Most everyone prayed, without hesitation, "Our Father, which art in heaven, hallowed be thy name. Thy kingdom come. Thy will be done, on earth as it is in heaven. Give us this day our daily bread, and forgive us our trespasses, as we forgive those who trespass against us. And lead us not into temptation, but deliver us from evil. For thine is the kingdom, and the power, and the glory forever. Amen."

As was his custom, Chuck wandered in the pulpit area a little as he spoke. *Ah, the wonders of a wireless microphone,* thought Ray. A few years back, a pastor that didn't stay behind the pulpit would be dragging a microphone cord behind him.

Chuck was several pounds slimmer now. Basketball was good exercise.

Chuck continued, "By the time I became a teen, I was pretty comfortable with praying. After all, prayer is basically just conversation with God. Even at an age in which I was nervous talking to girls or adults, I knew God was a friend who understood everything about me. I could talk to God as if he were right beside me."

Ray thought about his prayers as a teenager. There really wasn't much to think about, because he rarely prayed. Within a few months of the day he accepted Jesus as his savior, he had stopped praying at all. His place in heaven was secure, so he became just another teenager. Wow, a closer relationship with God would have made a big difference.

Chuck continued his introspection of his growing prayer life. Ray's mind wandered a little, as he thought about the years he'd drifted away from God. Maybe God would have made a big difference in his marriage. Maybe he wouldn't have married Dinah at all.

Living in Buckner was the best choice Ray had ever made. He'd gotten back in church, and back into a close relationship with God. "Love thy neighbor as thyself" had become not just a nice Jesus quote, but a lifestyle. God remade him, while he thought he was rebuilding himself.

Chuck got Ray's attention back when he wandered out of the pulpit area and down in front of the altar rail. "I've had some success in my prayer life, and I'll bet you have, too. God has answered some of my prayers for miraculous healings, and a straightening out of some knotty problems. Think for a minute, friends: Hasn't God also given you some amazing answers to prayer?"

Chuck paused for a few seconds, and Ray began thinking of his own answers to prayer. First and foremost was the healing of Debbie's broken finger. Then there was the answer to his prayer while driving south from picking up Mom's car, about giving him peace in a muddled situation.

The pastor continued with several examples of prayers of his that God had answered, some well-known by the congregation and some that were new revelations.

It was good to hear that he and Chuck were at similar places in their prayer life. Ray really liked the place he was at in this particular part of his life.

"I've talked a lot about myself today," Chuck said, "and I suspect you all have seen similarities in your own experience. Personally, though, I've got to change. You see, when I pray, I'm kind of selfish. I tell God what I want his answer to be. If somebody is ill, I want them healed, and the sooner the better. If they are in grief or anguish of any kind, I want God to eliminate that soon. I want everyone to be sheltered from adversity, though I know full well how trials and hard times can shape us into vessels of great use to God."

Chuck was back behind the pulpit now. He looked down and gave the pulpit a loud rap. "I've been trying to tell God how to do his business! Isn't that insane?"

The church building was completely quiet as the pastor slowly moved his gaze from person to person. A few shifted in their seats.

"The next big step in prayer for me is to get out of the driver's seat. I don't really want God to settle for my solutions. If I want big answers for my prayers, I've got to let God drive. Maybe I'll spend more of my prayer time praising God for what he has done, and for what he's about to do.

"So, thanks for listening this morning. That's where I am on my prayer journey. It's been a great walk with God, and the best is yet to come."

As the pianist played the last hymn, many chose to kneel at the altar to pray. Ray was one of them.

"Lord, I thought I'd gotten to a resting place. You have made me a better person, but I can see there's more work to do in building a better Raymond. Make all the changes you want to, Lord. I'm yours."

*****

ABOUT THE AUTHOR

Dennis Lanning grew up in upstate New York and attended Swarthmore College, near Philadelphia. After earning a B.S. degree in civil engineering, Dennis married Joy Josey. They moved to her native Georgia, where he worked in his father-in-law's grocery store for fourteen years.

God called Dennis into the ministry of the United Methodist Church, where he has served as a pastor since 1992. He has a Master of Divinity degree from Candler School of Theology at Emory University.

Dennis published his first novel, The Inside-Out Church, in 2014, through Tate Publishing. Circus on the Square, his second, came out in 2015. Early in 2018, Chips of Granite, a collection of short blogs, was published.

Dennis and Joy have a grown son, Paul, and a wonderful daughter-in-law, Nina. Paul and Nina have a daughter, Melanie.

Hobbies for Dennis include walking, pitching horseshoes, and playing basketball.